THE UNICORN RESCUE SOCIETY

SASQUATCH AND THE MUCKLESHOOT

THE UNICORN RESCUE SOCIETY
SASQUATCH AND THE MUCKLESHOOT

BY **Adam Gidwitz & Joseph Bruchac**

ILLUSTRATED BY **Hatem Aly**

CREATED BY **Jesse Casey, Adam Gidwitz, and Chris Lenox Smith**

DUTTON CHILDREN'S BOOKS

DUTTON CHILDREN'S BOOKS

Penguin Young Readers Group
An imprint of Penguin Random House LLC
375 Hudson Street
New York, NY 10014

Text & illustrations copyright © 2018 by Unicorn Rescue Society, LLC.

SL Lushootseed Style True Type font, courtesy of Tami Hohn,
© Puyallup Language Program.

CIP Data is available.

Printed in the United States of America

ISBN 9780735231764

1 3 5 7 9 10 8 6 4 2

Edited by Julie Strauss-Gabel
Design by Anna Booth
Text set in Legacy Serif ITC Std

This is a work of fiction. Names, characters, places, and incidents either are the product of the author's imagination or are used fictitiously, and any resemblance to actual persons, living or dead, businesses, companies, events, or locales is entirely coincidental.

To my wife, Nicola,
and all of those who care for the wild
—J.B.

To my wife, Lauren—
without whom none of my work would be possible
—A.G.

To Gado,
my childhood friend
—H.A.

UNICORNS ARE REAL.

At least, I think they are.

Dragons are definitely real. I have seen them. Chupacabras exist, too. Also Sasquatch. And mermaids—though they are *not* what you think.

But back to unicorns. When I, Professor Mito Fauna, was a young man, I lived in the foothills of Peru. One day, there were rumors in my town of a unicorn in danger, far up in the mountains. At that instant I founded the Unicorn Rescue Society—I was the only member—and set off to save the unicorn. When I finally located it, though, I saw that it was *not* a unicorn, but rather a qarqacha, the legendary two-headed llama of the Andes. I was very slightly disappointed. I rescued it anyway. Of course.

Now, many years later, there are members of the Unicorn Rescue Society all around the world. We are sworn to protect all the creatures of myth and legend. Including unicorns! If we ever find them! Which I'm sure we will!

But our enemies are powerful and ruthless, and we are in desperate need of help. Help from someone brave and kind and curious, and brave. (Yes, I said "brave" twice. It's important.)

Will you help us? Will you risk your very *life* to protect the world's mythical creatures?

Will you join the Unicorn Rescue Society?

I hope so. The creatures need you.

Defende Fabulosa! Protege Mythica!

Mito Fauna, DVM, PhD, EdD, etc.

CHAPTER ONE

U chenna Devereaux looked around the class-room.

Something was wrong.

All the usual kids were there. Jimmy, the big boy with the crew cut, had learned to fart to the tune of "Happy Birthday" over the weekend, and was showing his new skill to his pals Jasper and Johnna. They were singing along. Janey was staring out the window, digging into her nose with a finger—no, now two fingers. Pai Lu was wearing black eyeshadow, black nail polish, and black lipstick, and she sighed heavily as she read from a book of poetry by Algernon Swinburne called *A Ballad of Death.*

All of this was normal.

And yet, there was definitely something wrong. . . .

Their teacher, Miss Vole, was trying to teach them about trees. "Do you children know what an oak tree is?"

Uchenna sighed. Miss Vole always treated them like they were in kindergarten.

"An oak tree is one of the tallest trees here in New Jersey. But on the West Coast, in states like California, Oregon, and Washington—" She paused. "Have you heard of the West Coast, children?"

The lesson made Uchenna want to stick a pencil through her ear canal and into her brain. Which meant Elliot, her best friend and an expert on pretty much everything, was probably ready to throw himself through one of the hermetically sealed classroom windows. Uchenna glanced at him. . . .

Elliot! That's what was wrong. Where was Elliot?

Uchenna swiveled around in her chair, looking for Elliot Eisner, the only other kid in the school who was a member of the incredibly secret Unicorn Rescue Society. What happened to him? Why wasn't he in school? Was he sick? Had there been an accident? Maybe one of their enemies had captured him! Or was it—

BAM!

The door flew open, knocking three framed pictures off the wall.

Standing in the doorway was a tall man with a black-and-white beard, crazy hair, a threadbare tweed suit, and eyebrows that looked like something out of a science experiment.

"Buenos días, Miss Vole!" Professor Fauna exclaimed. Professor Fauna was the school social studies teacher. Everyone thought that he was a weirdo, and that he believed in unicorns, and that his office was a torture chamber under the

school. Only Uchenna and Elliot knew the truth: that he was definitely a weirdo, that he did believe in unicorns, and that his office under the school was not a torture chamber, but rather the headquarters of the Unicorn Rescue Society. "I am so sorry to interrupt you," Professor Fauna continued. "But I need to, ahem, borrow Elliot and Uchenna for a moment." His eyes landed on Uchenna, and his face lit up. He whispered to her, "It's about Bigfoot!" But because she was halfway across the room, his whisper was loud enough for everyone to hear.

"Did you just say it's about Bigfoot?" Pai Lu demanded, her words dripping with sarcasm.

Professor Fauna suddenly straightened up and looked very awkward. "Er . . . ah . . . um . . ." Everyone was staring at him. "Yes!" he said at last. "I did say Bigfoot! My big foot. You see, my right foot is bigger than my left. On the bottom of that big foot I have a horrible wart." The children all grimaced. "It is very painful," the professor went on. "And . . . and infected! So I need Elliot and Uchenna to help me!"

Miss Vole looked confused. "Why do you need Elliot and Uchenna to help you with your wart?"

"Right. Well . . . um . . . because . . . ," Professor Fauna stammered. "Because . . . I must drive to the doctor! But I cannot press upon the gas pedal because the wart is so painful! So one of them must do that for me while I drive. And . . . I have another wart on my thumb! So I cannot steer! So one of them will push the gas, and the other will steer, and I will sit in the driver's seat, telling them what to do."

Everyone stared at the professor, their mouths hanging open.

"It is no problem," Professor Fauna added. "We have done it before."

Finally, Miss Vole said, "Professor, that doesn't make any sense."

"*¡Mala palabra!* Am I not a teacher? Since when do teachers make sense? They are coming with me. Elliot, Uchenna, let's go." Then he looked around the room. "Wait, where is Elliot?"

Uchenna shrugged.

"Come! *¡Vámonos!* We will find him on the way!"

And with that, Professor Fauna turned and swept from the room. Uchenna hurried after him, glancing back at her class as she left.

Their mouths were still hanging open.

Then Jimmy farted the final two notes of "Happy Birthday."

CHAPTER TWO

Elliot Eisner poked his head out of the cafeteria.

He looked to the right, in the direction of his classroom. There was no one in the hallway. Perfect.

By dawdling, hanging back, and, finally, hiding behind one of the big cafeteria doors, he had waited just long enough to avoid the crush of the morning crowd. Crowds made him nervous. Actually, everything made him nervous. Even his best friend, Uchenna, made him nervous sometimes.

To be clear: Uchenna was awesome. She knew a ton about music, she always dressed like the lead singer in a punk rock band, and she didn't even mind that he obsessively read books like *Deadly Beasts of Kazakhstan.* And *Scottish Poisonous Snakes.* And *The Ten Thousand Worst Ways to Die*, volumes 1, 2, and 4 (volume 3 was missing from the public library).

Of all the things that made Elliot nervous, though, there was something that made him more nervous than anything else.

Actually, not something. Some*one*.

Elliot looked to the right again, down the hall, and then to the left, in the direction of the stairs that led to the subbasement. It was all clear. That certain someone was nowhere to be seen.

Perhaps it was going to be a good day. Perhaps he was finally going to do only normal stuff. Learn about something boring, like commas or trees. Not about supposedly mythical creatures that turn out to be real, like Jersey Devils and vicious dragons with magical saliva.

Not today, Elliot thought. Please let this be a boring day.

He shouldered his backpack and stepped cautiously out into the hall. Still nothing.

He began to walk toward the classroom. His shoes squeaked on the newly waxed floor.

No mythical creatures, he thought. No evil billionaires, no hazardous quests, no plane crashes. And not *him*. Please, not *him*.

Elliot glanced behind, at the stairs to the subbasement. Still clear. He turned toward the door of his classroom—

SMACK!

Elliot blinked. He was now staring at the ceiling, lying flat on the floor.

And *he* was looking down at Elliot. The one person in the world Elliot really did not want to see this morning. It was a wild-haired, black-and-white-bearded man with a very intense look on his face.

No, Elliot thought. Let this just be a bad dream. He closed his eyes, hoping that when he opened them again he would be waking up at home.

"Elliot!" Professor Fauna whispered. "This is no time for a nap! Come on!"

Elliot opened his eyes. Uchenna was grinning down at him.

She said, "We're going to rescue Bigfoot."

Elliot closed his eyes again, sighed, and said, "Of course."

CHAPTER THREE

Professor Fauna pushed open the doors of the school and marched toward the parking lot.

"Bigfoot?!" Elliot said, trying to keep up. "Seriously? Bigfoot doesn't even exist! That myth has been debunked hundreds of times!"

Uchenna was singing softly to herself:

𝄢 *What is a Bigfoot?*
    Do we even know?
    In the deepest winter, ♫

Is it white as fallen snow?
Living in the jungle,
Is it orange like an ape?
Hiding in your lunch box,
Is it purple like a grape?

Elliot looked at her. "I have to admit," he said, "that was one of your better songs."

Uchenna grinned.

"If Bigfoot is a myth, Elliot," Professor Fauna was saying, "why did I just get a call from Mack gəqidəb?"

"Mack guh-kay-dub?" said Uchenna, trying to pronounce the unfamiliar word. "That's an unusual name."

The professor raised an eyebrow. "You think so? I have known a number of people named Mack! There is even a tasty sandwich named that. Have you never heard of the Large Mack Donald?"

"I don't think that's what it's called."

"Anyway, Mack is a member of the

Muckleshoot Indian Nation. His name, gəqidəb, in Muckleshoot means 'bright minded.' His people live in the state of Washington. Now that is an unusual name, is it not? Washington? Why would someone name anything after two thousand pounds of laundry?" Professor Fauna shook his head. "Anyway, Mack and his family, like many of the Muckleshoot, are concerned about protecting the natural world . . . including creatures unrecognized by science!"

They had come to Professor Fauna's blue-and-white airplane, the *Phoenix*. It was in its usual three parking spots, between Principal Kowalski's seafoam-green hatchback and Miss Vole's Harley motorcycle.

A shiver skittered down Elliot's back. It was not just that the *Phoenix* was scarred with rust and dents, or that its front window was spider-webbed with cracks. It wasn't even that on their last flight, the plane had crashed. It was that, as Professor Fauna happily admitted, the *Phoenix*

crashed on every flight. But somehow the professor and his friends always got it flying again.
Elliot wished they would stop doing that.

Professor Fauna flung open the passenger
door of the small plane and helped Uchenna
in. Elliot hung back. Inside the plane, Uchenna
picked up a camouflage backpack with holes
poked all over the main compartment. She unzipped it. A small blue creature popped out. Its
head looked like the head of a tiny deer. A tiny
blue deer.

"Hey, Jersey," said Uchenna.

Jersey, the Jersey Devil, stood up in the bag and spread his bright red wings. Then he licked Uchenna's face.

Uchenna looked through the open airplane door at Elliot. "Aren't you coming?"

Elliot was staring at the *Phoenix* like it was trying to kill him. Which, as far as he was concerned, it was.

Suddenly, Jersey leaped from Uchenna's arms and glided on outstretched wings over to Elliot. The little blue creature dug his claws into Elliot's shirt. Then he licked Elliot on the nose.

Elliot sighed.

"Okay," he said. "Let's do this thing."

CHAPTER FOUR

The little plane careened down the school driveway toward the busy intersection, where trucks and buses rumbled across their path.

Imminent death, Elliot thought. Destruction. Doom. Disaster.

Of course he didn't say those words. He was too busy screaming.

At the last possible second, the professor yanked back on the yoke. The *Phoenix* zoomed

upward, grazing the top of an eighteen-wheeler truck.

"ALL RIGHT!" Uchenna whooped, over the panicked blast of the truck's horn.

Elliot stopped screaming. He was still terrified. He'd just run out of air in his lungs. He took a deep breath and considered whether he should start screaming again. He decided against it. He'd save his voice for the crash landing.

Uchenna gazed out the side window as the plane banked and headed west. Below them she

could see their school, the forest, and the smoke-
stacks of the Schmoke Industries power plant.
Jersey climbed up on her head for a better view.

The professor said, "Elliot, you said Bigfoot
was a myth."

Elliot exhaled. They were flying smoothly
now. He pushed back his mop of curly hair and sat
up straighter. Discussing mythical creatures with
Professor Fauna was one of his favorite things.

"I did. Every single photo or video has been
revealed as a fraud. Thousands of people search

for Bigfoot every year, and yet there's still no evidence that it exists."

"Ah . . . but, Elliot, surely you are aware of the common mistake you are making. A dearth of proof is not a proof of dearth."

"What's that supposed to mean?" Uchenna asked.

"For centuries," Professor Fauna said, flipping some switches on the dashboard of the little plane—switches that definitely did not do anything—"the scientists of Europe believed that giant apes of all kinds were myths. Orangutans, gorillas, even chimpanzees were unknown, and stories of hairy, manlike creatures in the jungles were thought to be only that— stories. The French believed that orangutans were merely humans living without the benefits of roads and toilets. *¡Qué raro!* Do I look like an orangutan to you?" Then Professor Fauna made a face like an orangutan.

Uchenna said, "Sorta?"

Professor Fauna ignored her. "Europeans encountered chimpanzees only four hundred years ago! And, until very recently, they didn't even realize that there are two different species of chimpanzees: chimps and bonobos."

Just then, Uchenna noticed that the sky was turning black and the clouds were getting thicker. She nudged Elliot. But he was too engrossed in Professor Fauna's lecture. Jersey had curled up in Elliot's lap and fallen asleep.

"The case of the gorilla is truly interesting," the professor went on, now completely ignoring the sky and the airplane's controls. "There

were reports more than two thousand years ago about giant apes in tropical Africa, twice as big as a human! But, until 1847, scientists believed

that the gorilla was no more than a story! That is barely a hundred and fifty years ago!"

The little plane was starting to shake as it entered the black clouds. Uchenna said, "Elliot, have you checked your—"

"Shhh," Elliot hushed her.

"I need to learn this before we meet Mack ɡəqidəb and the Muckleshoot."

"All over the world," the professor went on, "there are stories of giant ape creatures. There are the yeti of the Himala-yas, the orang pendek of Indone-sia, the yowie in Australia. . . . If the gorilla was discovered only a hundred fifty years ago, might

not all of these apelike creatures exist?"

"Maybe," said Elliot. "But—"

"Elliot," Uchenna interrupted, tightening her seat belt. "You'd better—"

"Uchenna," Elliot said, "can it wait just one min—"

Suddenly, a massive gust of wind hit the plane so hard that the *Phoenix* turned upside down. Elliot found himself pasted to the roof of the little aircraft and then, as the plane righted itself, back in his seat. "Gunnnh," he groaned.

Uchenna reached over. "Your seat belt's not on." She strapped her friend in.

Elliot muttered, "Thank you," and closed his eyes.

CHAPTER FIVE

A few hours later, the *Phoenix* started to rumble and rattle.

Elliot and Uchenna had fallen asleep on each other, with Jersey stretched out between their laps. But all three jerked awake at the sudden turbulence.

"Are we there?" Uchenna asked, wiping her eyes with her sleeve. "Will we be on the ground soon?"

"No and yes," Professor Fauna replied. "No,

we are not quite there. We seem to be about three hundred miles south of our intended destination."

Elliot stretched his arms above his head. "What's the 'yes' part then?"

"Yes, we will be on the ground soon because we are out of gas."

Elliot shot a panicked look at Uchenna.

"Don't worry!" Professor Fauna held up his cell phone. "I have informed Mack, and he is driving down from Washington to meet us."

Uchenna looked down at the forest ahead of them. "Those trees are big," she said.

"They look like Douglas firs," Elliot said. "Some of the oldest are thirteen hundred years old and over three hundred feet tall." He suddenly turned on Professor Fauna. "We're not going to try to land there, right?"

"Ah . . . ," Fauna said, as the plane's engine began to sputter. "Not exactly . . . You see, there is another very small problem."

"Which is what?" asked Elliot.

"We lost our landing gear when we hit that truck on takeoff."

"WHAT?"

"Sooooo," Professor Fauna said, pulling hard on the yoke to level the plane into a glide, "we are not going to land among the Douglas firs. We are going to crash among the Douglas firs."

Elliot grabbed Uchenna, who grabbed Jersey, who grabbed Elliot's face. Elliot screamed.

And the plane plummeted into the trees.

CHAPTER SIX

Smashing into the heavy branches of the giant fir trees knocked both wings off the plane. It also tossed Uchenna, Elliot, Jersey, and the professor out of the little aircraft's cockpit.

But rather than tumbling down toward the earth with the rest of the wreckage of the *Phoenix*, splintering branches as they fell and probably ending up like shish kebabs, they all found themselves lying on their backs, on a wide canvas platform, staring up through the green needles of a Douglas fir at the blue sky.

None of them moved for a moment. They felt the gentle swaying of the tree in the wind, heard the tree groaning as it swayed, and smelled the clean smell of fir needles.

"This might be kinda relaxing," Elliot said at last, "if we hadn't just been in a plane crash." He rolled onto his stomach. "Also, we appear to be hundreds of feet in the air. I take it back. This is not relaxing at all."

"I love it," Uchenna murmured, breathing in and out with the swaying of the tree. "But how did we not just die?"

Jersey lay on his back beside her and gave a tiny, contented sigh.

Stretching next to the canvas platform and the enormous tree trunk were steel cables that rose high above them and descended past the platform to the ground. Professor Fauna got to his knees and started hoisting something up from below. "The scientists who are studying these great trees," he said, "place platforms like these all around this forest to observe the unique ecosystem of the Douglas fir. Having been here once before, I saw this platform and aimed for it."

"That is unbelievable," said Elliot. "Like, literally unbelievable."

Professor Fauna shrugged. "I may be bad at landing, but at least I have excellent aim." He continued pulling at the steel cables. "These trees! They provide food and shelter for so many

creatures. They hold the soil in place and store moisture. Cut them down, and even the salmon in nearby rivers die, because soil erodes and spills into the water." The professor inhaled the sweet scent of the treetops. "These firs are the guardians of life. It is something that the original people of this land have always understood. People such as our friend Mack. Who is surely waiting for us below."

"He's waiting below this exact tree?" Uchenna asked.

"Of course!" the professor answered. Just then, a belt with several straps on it rose into sight, attached to the cables that Professor Fauna had been hoisting up. "Hold this," he said to Uchenna, handing her one. He then pulled two more such contraptions toward him. "Our fellow member of the Unicorn Rescue Society sent these harnesses up the tree for us to use."

The professor strapped himself into one of the harnesses. "There is one for each of us."

Elliot required a bit of help putting his on because his hands were shaking. But soon all three were strapped in.

"¡*Magnífico!*" Fauna said. "Now, you put one foot in the stirrup, loosen this up here with your hands, press down with your foot, and *¡ya está!*"

And, just like that, the professor was lifted two feet in the air. And he swung out over the abyss.

"Now you, children!" Fauna called to them.

"No," said Elliot. "No. No. No. Absolutely not."

Uchenna put her hand on Elliot's shoulder. "We'll do it together."

Elliot was shaking, but he closed his eyes and nodded.

They prepared the harnesses, and then Uchenna said, "One . . . two . . . three!"

Elliot and Uchenna pushed down with their feet and felt themselves both lifting up and swinging out.

"WOOO-HOOOO!" Uchenna shouted.

Elliot opened his eyes. They were dangling to-gether, the three of them like puppets on strings, far, far above the forest floor. Something whizzed by their faces. It was Jersey, joyfully gliding in cir-cles around them.

"But we just went up," Uchenna said to the professor. "How do we go down?"

The professor smiled at her. "Simple. Grasp here to loosen the tension and you will slide quickly down. It will feel like flying. To stop, just let go. Observe."

The professor grabbed a strap under his thigh—and plummeted down. Elliot's stomach went with him.

"I was right before," Elliot said. "No. No. No."

Uchenna didn't notice. An idea for a new song had just hit her.

What's the difference
Between falling and flying?
Swooping and whooping,

Out of the sky-ing.
See how we're soaring?
We're not even trying!
I know I'm in love
With the feeling of flying!

"Uchenna . . . ," Elliot said.

"That was another good one, right?" Uchenna asked. "It was in the style of Rodgers and Hammerstein." Then she said, "We've got this, Elliot."

Elliot nodded uneasily.

"Grab the release, okay?"

"Okay . . ."

"One, two . . . threEEEEEEEEE!"

CHAPTER SEVEN

Elliot and Uchenna dropped like stones. It was the most awful feeling. It was also wonderful. He was going to die. He was flying. He . . .

"LET GO!" Uchenna yelled.

Elliot released his grip. The cable caught, bounced him up, and then he felt his toes touching the ground.

"I am not dead," he said, as Professor Fauna and Uchenna helped him out of the harness. "I am NOT dead." He dropped to his knees and pressed his face against the sweet-smelling moss at his feet.

"Can we do that again?" Uchenna asked.

Elliot looked around. The only signs of human activity, aside from the climbing cables, were the scattered pieces of the *Phoenix*. There were huge-trunked trees everywhere. Jersey, who had landed gracefully on the pine-needle-strewn ground, scampered over to another enormous tree and began climbing it, his front claws gripping the bark and his wings flapping, as his back hooves clopped against the wood. Then, when he was about twenty feet off the ground, he launched himself off the trunk and glided through the quiet forest air, disappearing and reappearing as

he went through the shadows of the huge trees.

The trees were so big that you could hide a house behind one of them. Or other big things. Which re-minded Elliot: "Are there bears here?"

"Ah yes," Professor Fauna replied. "This forest is fine ursine habitat. Excellent for bears. Mostly the black bear. Which is very dangerous, though perhaps not as deadly as its brown cousin, the grizzly."

"Aw," groaned Uchenna. "I wanna see a griz-zly bear."

"No, you do not," Elliot replied. "A grizzly bear could—"

Suddenly, a huge, hairy brown bear lurched out from behind a tree.

This time both Elliot and Uchenna screamed.

"Play dead!" Elliot shouted, pushing Uchenna under him as he fell to the ground. He stretched out over Uchenna, bravely putting his body between her and the huge, hairy beast looming above them.

He peeked out of the corner of one eye at the grizzly.

On closer inspection, it didn't seem to be a grizzly after all. It was more like a big, brown gorilla . . . though it stood upright . . . and its legs extended down to two huge, hairy . . .

Bigfoot! It was Bigfoot!

And it was going to kill them.

Elliot watched in horror as Bigfoot reached up—and removed its own head.

Which made Elliot scream again.

And then Elliot watched in utter confusion as Professor Fauna picked his way over him and Uchenna to the headless Bigfoot and reached out his hand.

The tall man in the Bigfoot costume took the professor's hand and shook it vigorously.

"Children," said the professor, "why do you keep trying to take naps? Get up! Allow me to

introduce Mack gəqidəb, our member of the Unicorn Rescue Society with the Muckleshoot Nation. Mack, meet Uchenna and Elliot."

Mack reached out his hands to pull them both up to their feet and said, "kʷədačiʔc." It sounded something like "kwuh-dah-cheets."

Both children looked at him uncertainly.

Mack grinned. "Never heard Muckleshoot before? I just said 'Shake hands with me' in my language. Pleased to meet you. Your name is Uchenna, pronounced Ooo-CHEN-ah?"

Uchenna nodded.

"Good," Mack said with a chuckle. "If it was pronounced UH-chen-ah, it would mean something like 'too bad' in Muckleshoot. Which really would be too bad." He grinned. "Anyhow, I liked what you were singing up there in the tree. Maybe we should call you Sings Real Sweet."

Uchenna blushed. "That'd be nice." She smiled.

"And you're Elliot?" Mack asked. Elliot

nodded. "Maybe we'll call you Screams A Lot." Elliot's shoulders drooped. Mack laughed. "Aw, don't take it too hard. Your screaming was even louder than the *Phoenix* hitting the top of that tree. We can always tell when you arrive, Professor, by the sound of the plane crash."

Mack took off the rest of his costume, including the heavy boots that left prints like two enormous bare feet, and a pair of huge hairy gloves. "Here," Mack said, tossing one of the gloves to the professor. "Let me give you a hand."

Elliot and Uchenna looked uncertainly at Professor Fauna.

"He is always making jokes like this," the professor explained.

"You didn't think it was punny?" Mack asked. "Oh, well." He ran a hand through his black hair, and Elliot noticed a thick silver ring on his finger, marked with a unicorn. The signet ring of the Unicorn Rescue Society.

"My truck's parked thataway," Mack said. "Come on."

"Wait a minute," Uchenna said. "Why were you dressed up like a huge hairy monster? Is that what Bigfoot really is, just people wearing ape suits? Is Bigfoot not real?"

Mack shook his head. "That's right," he said. "Bigfoot is just a myth."

"Oh!" Elliot sighed. "Thank heavens. Now we can go home and forget all about—"

Mack held up his hand. "Nope. Bigfoot, like I said, is a myth. Sasquatch, on the other hand, is very real."

CHAPTER EIGHT

Mack's truck was a surprise. Uchenna had never seen anything like it before. It looked as if it had been put together from parts of several different vehicles. It had the bed of a full-size pickup truck, the passenger interior of a minivan, and the front end of a 1950s Cadillac. It was all the same color—more or less. Each part had its own unique shade of green, from discreet camouflage to dark khaki to a bright, eye-catching kelly. Instead of the standard two or four doors, it had seven. And because its various parts took up so much space, it was almost as long as a bus.

As Elliot stood there staring, Uchenna looked under the truck. Yup, it had seven tires. Not only that, it had something like a smokestack sticking out of the back. There was an odor coming from it that was sort of familiar and pleasant. What was that smell?

Mack chuckled. "I call it the TruckVanAc. Part truck, part van, part Cadillac. Did you know it's one of a kind? I put this baby together myself."

"Hard to believe . . . ," Elliot murmured. He wondered if riding in it would be like flying in the *Phoenix*, with parts falling off as they chugged along.

"My friend Mack," Professor Fauna said, "is a great mechanical genius. He holds engineering degrees from the Rensselaer Polysyllabic Institution and the Massachusetts Institute of Technophobia."

"Close enough, Professor." Mack patted the

hood of the TruckVanAc. Nothing fell off, which reassured Elliot, slightly. "All recycled parts," he said, stroking his chin. "How many miles per gallon of gas do you think this gets?"

"Five?" Elliot guessed.

Mack's smile broadened as he shook his head.

"Twenty?" Uchenna ventured.

Mack shook his head again. "Nope," he said. "The answer is none. No gas at all."

Uchenna snapped her fingers. "I've got it!" she said. "That's french fry grease I smell!"

Mack laughed out loud. "You've got a good

nose there, Sings Real Sweet. This baby runs on used cooking oil I pick up from fast-food joints. They give it to me for free since it saves them the trouble of shipping it off to the dump. Back when I was in my senior year at the Massachusetts Institute of Technology, we took a car all the way from Boston to Los Angeles on grease alone. Modified injector nozzles, stronger glow plugs, parallel fuel filters. Got us thirty-seven miles per gallon on vegetable oil. Now TruckVanAc here, thanks to a few of my own ideas, gets one hundred miles per gallon. Runs quiet and burns clean—aside from smelling like a Big Mac. Which suits me fine, eh? Mack in his Big Mac TruckVanAc!"

Professor Fauna tapped Mack on the shoulder. "So, speaking of french fries . . . ," he said. "I am feeling rather hungry."

Mack motioned to the TruckVanAc. "Come on," he said. "We'll get some food when I refill at this burger place I know up in Portland."

CHAPTER NINE

"So, you're a member of the Muckleshoot Tribe . . . ," Uchenna said as they pulled out from the forest access road and onto the main highway. Elliot had to move a hard hat and a fluorescent-orange vest from his seat to the floor. He tried not to step on them.

Mack nodded.

"So . . . ," said Uchenna. "Muckleshoot . . ."

Mack grinned. "You probably want to know about our name, huh?"

"Sure! That is, if you want to tell us," Uchenna said.

"We didn't used to be called that," Mack told them. "We used to be two different Nations: Duwamish and Upper Puyallup. Our people lived all the way from Puget Sound to the crest of the Cascade Mountains. We fished and hunted and gathered and took care of the natural world for thousands of years before Europeans started arriving." Mack shook his head. "We welcomed them, but they kept taking more and more of our land. The United States Army kept showing up and telling us to move. Eventually, we signed treaties giving up most of our territory in exchange for a small reservation—on an old army base called Muckleshoot. They started calling us that, and the name stuck."

Mack sighed. "The treaty was supposed to guarantee us our rights to hunt and fish and gather in all our old spots. But the federal government broke every promise to us, forbidding us from even hunting and fishing where we had for thousands of years."

"That's awful!" Uchenna exclaimed.

"Yup," Mack agreed. "Just as bad, they forbade us from performing our rituals. They took kids away from their homes and sent them to boarding schools where they were punished for speaking their own language."

"What?!" exclaimed Elliot. He looked like he might cry. "Why? Why would they do that?"

Mack sighed. "Because white folks believed Native cultures were primitive and our culture was holding us back. They believed the white way of life was superior—they really thought that. They figured that the best thing was to force us to give up our languages and our customs and take us away from our families. You know what they called it? 'Kill the Indian and save the man.'"

"That's horrible!" Uchenna cried.

Professor Fauna added, "Today this is called cultural genocide."

They all stared out the TruckVanAc's windows, trying to imagine what it would be like to have the government take you away from your family and try to kill your language, your beliefs, and your traditions.

Finally, Uchenna broke the silence. "Are things any better now?"

Mack grinned. "You bet, Sings Real Sweet. The Muckleshoot started protesting, and we took our case to court. We won our fishing rights back, and from then on, our economy came roaring back. We started our own seafood products company, a tree farm, built a racetrack, the White River Amphitheatre—"

"Wait," Uchenna interrupted. "The White River Amphitheatre was built by the Muckleshoot?"

"Yes," said Mack. "You've heard of it?"

"Are you kidding? Just this summer you guys had Weezer, the Pixies, Counting Crows, and G-Eazy! Oh, and Foreigner!" Uchenna started singing, "You're as cold as ice! Ba-dum-DUM! / You're willing to sac-ri-fice our looooove—"

"Annnnyway . . . ," Mack went on, "a lot of the revenue that allows us to do all this comes from our casino—which is the biggest in the state. Two thousand people work there now, including plenty of local folks who aren't tribal members. We spend the money we make at the casino on economic development, housing, tons on our schools, and—my favorite part—buying back land that was stolen from us all those years ago."

"Yay!" said Elliot. "That sounds good!"

"You have no idea. A few years ago, we bought back Sasquatch Valley."

"Is that where . . . ?" Elliot began.

"You bet, little buddy. It's where the sasquatch live."

Professor Fauna cut in. "That was when Mack and I became friends. He told me that they bought the land to protect these magnificent creatures. And I invited him to join the Unicorn Rescue Society."

"*Defende Fabulosa!*" said Mack.

"*Protege Mythica!*" the professor replied.

"But now the sasquatch are in trouble?" Uchenna asked.

Mack nodded. Just then, he flipped his turn signal—which flashed like a neon sign—and started a wide, slow turn into the parking lot of a little joint called Bigfoot Burgers. "Let's fuel up, and then I'll tell you all about it."

CHAPTER TEN

The parking lot of Bigfoot Burgers was mostly empty, except for the TruckVanAc and a white van with a small satellite dish on top. Emblazoned on the side of the van were the letters SNERT TV. Below the red letters were the words: ALL THE NEWS WE WANT YOU TO KNOW.

Jersey had fallen asleep during the ride, so Uchenna gently slid him into her backpack. Mack opened his door.

"WAIT!" Professor Fauna hissed. They all froze. Jersey woke up and made a grumpy sound.

"What is it, Mito?" Mack asked.

Professor Fauna pointed out the window of the TruckVanAc. "Do you see this van? The one that says SNERT?"

"Yeah," said Mack. "It's a news van. This place has been crawling with them. That's one of the reasons I called you—"

"No!" the professor interrupted. "This is not just any news van! It is part of the new channel Schmoke News, Entertainment, and Retail Television."

"Don't they already own a network?" Elliot asked. "Lowest Common Denominator or something?"

"I love LCD!" Uchenna replied.

"You do?"

"Yeah! They've got so many great shows! *My Pet's Got Talent, Can Your Grandma Dance Like My Grandma?*, and those awesome detective shows: *Investigation: Houston*; *Investigation: Duluth*; and *Investigation: Saw Pit, Colorado*." Uchenna paused. "Actually, that last one is kinda slow."

"You're weird," Elliot said.

Uchenna shrugged.

Professor Fauna waved away the children's commentary. "Yes, yes, but they have started a cable news channel. And now their news van is here!"

"That news van has been stalking everyone around here for weeks," said Mack. "They keep asking questions about Bigfoot and sasquatch and the Abominable Snowman and any other hairy ape they can find on the internet. Careful what you say in there—"

"I am always careful!" Professor Fauna announced.

Mack looked at the kids. They both rolled their eyes.

"Yeah, I'm tempted to leave him in the Truck-VanAc," Mack said.

Elliot began nodding vigorously. The professor announced, "My lips are peeled!"

"That's what I'm worried about," Mack murmured. But they all clambered out of the TruckVanAc and made their way across the parking lot and through the swinging door of Bigfoot Burgers.

CHAPTER ELEVEN

Bigfoot Burgers was a quaint little shack decked out completely in Bigfoot merchandise. Stuffed Bigfoot dolls, overpriced T-shirts (MY FAMILY SAW BIGFOOT AND ALL I GOT WAS THIS DUMB SHIRT), and a display of Bigfoot Bars, which were gooey nut bars wrapped in cellophane, selling for $4.95 apiece.

As Mack walked into the restaurant, a man standing behind a counter wearing a white apron called out, "Hey, Chief! I got that oil set aside for ya out back."

"Thanks, Senator," Mack replied.

The man looked confused. "Uh . . . yer welcome," he said, and walked back into the kitchen.

Mack turned to Uchenna and Elliot. "That happens a lot," said Mack, shaking his head. "But not every Indian is a chief."

"Just like not every white guy is a senator?" Uchenna said.

"You got it, Sings Real Sweet."

An older woman with hanging jowls, granny glasses, and an apron emblazoned with the words BIGFOOT'S BEST BUDDY asked if they wanted anything.

"Can we get some fries for our hungry friends here?" Mack asked her. Then he turned to Professor Fauna. "I'll be out back filling up the TruckVanAc."

Mack walked into the kitchen and out of sight. Professor Fauna, Elliot, and Uchenna clambered up on stools at the counter. Just then, the front door swung open and a skinny guy with glasses and acne-covered cheeks hurried in, eating a Bigfoot Bar.

"Hey!" yelled the woman behind the register. "No outside food!"

"But I just bought this in here!" said the skinny guy.

"Yeah, but then you took it outside, didn't you?"

"But—"

"So now it's outside food. You want another one? Four ninety-five."

The skinny guy's shoulders slumped. He put the bar in his pocket and slouched past the register.

Elliot and Uchenna watched him make his way to a booth in the corner. A stunning blond woman in a bright blue dress was already in that

booth. She had long, black eyelashes and lipstick
so red it could have stopped traffic at an intersection. Across from her was a heavyset, balding guy.
There was a huge camera on the table. The skinny
guy with the acne tried to sit next to the woman.
There was much more room on her side of the
booth. But she shook her head and said, "This
side is for the talent, Sam."

Sam Brounsnout, producer, crammed himself in next to the cameraman.

"Well, I just got off the phone with the bosses," he said. "They want us to keep looking."

"Keep looking!" the blond woman exclaimed. "We've been looking for two weeks! I'm Grace Goodwind! I don't go tramping around in the woods for two weeks with no story, no leads, no prime time! What do you think I am? A journalist?"

"Aren't you . . . ?" Sam mumbled.

"No! I'm a TV reporter. It's not the same thing." She tossed her long hair. It looked, momentarily, like she was in a shampoo commercial. "Bigfoot isn't even real! How long are we going to look for something that doesn't exist?"

Sam sighed. "I don't know, Ms. Goodwind. The bosses said—"

"Ugh. Who cares about the bosses?"

The cameraman said, "Well, I, for one, would like to get paid."

"Stow it, Jerry," muttered Grace Goodwind.

"It's Andy," the cameraman replied. "We've

worked together for a year and a half. Back at LCD. And before that, when you were on local—"

Grace cut him off with a growl. "Never. Mention. Local."

Suddenly, a shriek shattered the calm of the burger joint. And then a bellow: "WHO STOLE MY BIGFOOT BARS?"

Everyone froze. The woman with the granny glasses was pointing at the box on the counter. A box that was now empty.

CHAPTER TWELVE

The owner came rushing out of the back. "What's wrong, Ma?"

"My Bigfoot Bars are gone!" she announced.

"Those bars," Uchenna whispered to Elliot. "They're sort of like the ones your mom and grandma make."

"Yeah," said Elliot. "So?"

"So, isn't Jersey obsessed with those bars?"

A motion from above caught their eyes. They looked up and saw the little Jersey Devil sitting on the head of a wooden Bigfoot statue, happily munching on a Bigfoot Bar.

"Oh no . . ."

Uchenna hissed at Professor Fauna, "Professor, hand me the backpack."

The professor quietly handed it over. Unfortunately, neither he nor Uchenna realized that the backpack's food compartments were unzipped—and two dozen Bigfoot bars went spilling out onto the floor.

"There!" the owner's mother yelled. "There they are! That strange man STOLE them!"

Professor Fauna backed up against a wall. From the booth in the corner, Elliot heard Grace Goodwind shout, "Doug, roll the film! This could be good!" She slid out of her seat, grabbed a mic from Andy's camera bag, and pulled up to her full, imposing height. She straightened her

blue dress with a couple of expert flicks and tugs, shook out her shampoo-commercial-quality hair, and said, "On me!"

As the owner of Bigfoot Burgers and his mother advanced on Professor Fauna, Ms. Goodwind began to report:

"Grace Goodwind, here. Reporting from . . . what's the name of this dump?" she hissed at Sam, the producer. "Never mind, who cares . . . Reporting from some pit stop in Portland, Oregon."

Meanwhile, Professor Fauna was trying to

persuade the owner and his mother to not call the police.

"You see, I did not steal them. . . . They were stolen, yes. But not by me . . . Yes, they were in the backpack that I was carrying. But that evidence is just circumstantial! . . . Who stole them? Well . . . uh . . ." Professor Fauna looked at the Jersey Devil, sitting on top of the wooden Bigfoot's head. The owner and his mother followed his gaze.

"WHAT IN BIGFOOT'S NAME IS THAT?" the mother shouted.

"Sandy! Get that on film!" Grace shrieked.

But just as Andy panned to Jersey, Elliot pushed the Bigfoot statue over. The owner bellowed, his mother screamed, Professor Fauna scooped up the backpack, Uchenna grabbed Jersey, and Elliot sprinted for the door.

They burst into the bright parking lot just as Mack pulled the TruckVanAc around.

"She's all filled up. I should go in there and

'tank' them," he added, grinning. "Don't you think?"

"No time for jokes!" Uchenna exclaimed, throwing open the door and tossing Jersey inside. Everyone piled in after her, just as the restaurant door burst open and Grace Goodwind, Sam, and Andy appeared. Andy was trying to get his camera back on his shoulder. "Did you get that? Did you get it?" Grace was shrieking.

"I don't think so," Andy answered. "The kid pushed over the Bigfoot just before I could get it in focus!"

"What's happening?" asked Mack.

"JUST GO!" Uchenna shouted.

Mack gunned the engine and roared out of the parking lot.

"What was that thing?" Sam asked, as they watched the TruckVanAc peel out onto Route 101.

"Looked like part truck, part van, part Cadillac," Andy answered.

"No, I meant that blue creature with wings."

"I know exactly what it is," Grace whispered.

"You do? What?"

"That," she said, her painted red lips bending into a smile, "is my prime-time story."

As the TruckVanAc hauled up Route 101 toward the Washington State line, Mack turned to the kids.

"Did that cameraman say you knocked over my Bigfoot statue?"

"That's your Bigfoot statue?"

"Well, I carved it."

"It was pretty good."

"Was?"

Elliot and Uchenna looked at each other and winced. Elliot said, "Remember how you took off the head of your Bigfoot costume when we first met?"

"Sure . . ."

"Well, have you ever heard of foreshadowing?"

Mack sighed.

CHAPTER THIRTEEN

Elliot had meant to ask Mack to continue his story about why he needed their help, but once they were safely out of sight of the news crew at Bigfoot Burgers, his eyes grew heavy. The long plane ride across the continent, the crash landing in the tree, the drive to Portland, and then the burger joint fiasco had exhausted him. And he wasn't the only one.

Before long, only Mack—shaking his head and smiling—was awake. The TruckVanAc was

filled with a symphony of snores, from Fauna's raspy bass rumble, to Elliot's bagpipe-like tenor, to Uchenna's musical alto, to the delicate soprano trill coming from Jersey's little snout.

Mack steered the TruckVanAc from outside of Portland, Oregon, to just south of Seattle, Washington, and not a single one of his passengers stirred. It was not until the big vehicle's seven wheels went *ka-thudd-ka-thudd-thudd-*

thudd-thudd-thudd-thudd that Elliot was jerked awake.

"AGGHH!" he shouted, trying to leap out of his seat belt. "We're crashing!!!"

Mack reached out and grabbed his shoulder. "Calm down, Panics Easily," Mack said. "That was just us driving over a cattle guard."

"Sorry," Elliot said with a sigh. "I was dreaming of the *Phoenix*."

"Yeah, just seeing that thing on the ground gives me nightmares," Mack agreed.

"Are we there?" Uchenna asked, rubbing her eyes and looking out the window. They were on an unpaved road in a forest. None of the moss-covered trees were as gigantic as the Douglas firs down in Oregon, but they were still way bigger than anything in New Jersey.

"Just about," Mack said. "We're in the tribal forest. My place is up around the next bend."

Sure enough, as they topped a ridge and rounded a hill, there it was in front of them.

"Good gracious!" Elliot exclaimed. Uchenna just stared.

Perched on a crest looking over a wide, wooded valley was a huge, two-story structure made with a stone foundation and walls of big logs. There were balconies and wide windows facing east on both floors, and solar panels on part of the roof. The rest of the broad roof, which was slightly slanted, was covered with earth. Half was fenced in, and Uchenna could see that it held a beautiful vegetable garden with pathways through it. The other half was planted with small fruit trees and berry bushes. Yes, there was a garden and an orchard on the roof.

But the most amazing thing about the house was that the logs weren't lying on their sides, stacked on top of one another, like in most log cabins. No, these stood upright. And every single log had been carved into the shapes of all sorts of animals: turtles at the bottom; bears and wolves and raccoons above them; and birds of prey like hawks and eagles on top.

They all got out and walked toward the house. "This," Uchenna said, gaping, "is super cool. They're like totem poles."

"Yup. They're not technically totem poles," Mack explained. "Because you wouldn't use a totem pole to build a house. You'd put them out front to tell a story or to memorialize something. But once I get my pal Jane Saw working, sometimes I get a little carried away."

"Who's Jane Saw?" Elliot asked. And then he said, "Wait. Never mind. I get it."

Mack grinned. "Every one of those logs tells a story." He looked up toward the roof. "There's Raven."

Elliot nodded. He'd read an interesting book of Native American stories called *Raven Steals the Light*. "The trickster hero, right?"

"Not exactly," Mack said. "In this case I mean Raven, my—Look out!"

Mack's warning came a second too late. A shape suddenly came leaping down from the roof. *THUD!*

Elliot found himself on the ground with a girl wearing glasses sitting on his chest. She was about his size and dressed entirely in green camouflage. Her dark hair was woven into three long braids, tied with strips of fur.

"I'm Raven," she said. "Who are you?"

"Uh," Elliot said, trying to catch his breath. "Uh . . . huh . . . huh . . ."

"Pleased to meet you, Uhhuhhuh," Raven said. She looked up at Mack. "He's cute, Pop. Can I keep him?"

"No. And actually," Mack added, "his name is not Uhhuhhuh. It's Screams A Lot."

"No," Elliot managed to grunt. "It's . . . Elliot."

Mack reached down one big hand to pick up Raven.

"Folks," he said, as Elliot scrambled to his feet, "meet my daughter, Raven. Raven, these are my fellow members of the Unicorn Rescue Society."

"haʔɫ labdubuɫəd ti dsyəyaʔyaʔ—it's nice to see you, my friends," Raven said.

"Kwuh-dah-cheets," Uchenna answered.

"Wow," Raven said. "That was almost Muckleshoot."

"That was how your father greeted us. Sort of," Uchenna replied. "Maybe you can teach me how to say it right?"

"You bet," Raven said. She reached out to shake Uchenna's hand, and then paused. "Do you like music?"

"I live for it," Uchenna answered.

"What kind?"

"Blues, folk, techno, hard rock, pop, emo, country . . ."

Raven made a face. "My thing is hip-hop."

"Like who? J. Cole? Nikki? Or old-school? Latifah is great. So is Tribe. But—"

Raven laughed. "We're going to be friends." Then she said, "What is that?"

Jersey was scrambling around on the ground, going berserk over something that no one else could see. He looked like he was doing some kind of hyper-caffeinated aerobics.

"That's a Jersey Devil," Uchenna said. "His name is Jersey, but I wanted to call him Bonechewer."

"Bonechewer is a better name," Raven agreed.

Mack said, "I think I know what's driving the little guy crazy. Do I smell salmon cooking?"

By now, it really looked like Jersey was doing jumping jacks.

"On the back deck grill, Pops," Raven said.

So they all went inside for dinner, before Jersey hurt himself.

CHAPTER FOURTEEN

After Mack had given thanks in Muckleshoot to the salmon for the gift of its life, Raven began filling everyone's plates. Jersey got one, too, which he ate ferociously, and then came up whining for more, which Raven happily fed to him, piece by piece. After the meal, Jersey calmed down, and they all sat and looked out on the beautiful wooded valley. A bald eagle coasted over the tops of the pines, its body framed by the golden light.

"It looks like a postcard," Elliot murmured.

"To you, it's a postcard," Mack replied. "To us, it is our home."

"*Amigo mío,*" Fauna said, "please explain now why we are here."

Mack nodded and leaned back in his chair. "Our family has a long history with sasquatch. Of all the forest people, the sasquatch have always been the most elusive. More so since white folks showed up here with their guns three centuries ago. Sasquatch are big and strong. Even grizzly bears wouldn't challenge 'em. But a gun is a whole different thing."

Elliot raised his hand. "Uh, Mr. gəqidəb, are there grizzly bears here?"

"Nope. They're all gone now, every one of them killed by guns. But even when those bears were here, they would run from a sasquatch."

Elliot raised his hand again.

Mack chuckled. "Listen, Million And One Questions. I know you've got lots you want to ask. But folks often forget that we have two ears and only one mouth for a reason. We should listen twice as much as we talk. Hang in there just a bit longer, and I might answer your questions before you ask them. Okay?"

Elliot put his hands in his lap and nodded.

Mack smiled and nodded back. "Sasquatch may be big and strong, but they hardly ever hurt people. They even help people sometimes. Listen to this."

Mack inhaled through his nose, his shoulders rising. The sun shone on his black hair.

"When I was about four years old I was out with my parents, walking through these woods." Mack pointed with his chin. "My parents were walking ahead of me, talking about something or other, and I was dawdling. Taking it all in. I found an interesting stone on the ground. And then another one. And another. I stepped back. They looked like they had been placed there, like an arrow, pointing deeper into the woods.

"Well, I forgot all about my parents, and they must have forgotten all about me. I went the way those stones were pointing, and after a little while, I came to a little gully, surrounded by fallen logs and thick branches. I pushed through the brush—and found the most amazing thing I'd ever seen in my young life."

Elliot opened his mouth to guess what it was and then quickly shut it again. Mack nodded approvingly.

"There was a family of sasquatch, lounging in the falling light," he said. "A huge male was leaning against a rock, and a little one was winding long tendrils of moss through the big male's sleek brown hair. A female was nursing a little baby sasquatch, while another female— maybe her sister—was crouched over an anthill,

sliding a stick into it and then licking ants off the stick.

"I guess it was because I was just a little guy at the time, but I wasn't scared at all. And neither were the sasquatch. The male just looked at me. The female with the stick stood up. Even though she had been crouching like an ape, she stood upright, straight as a human and taller than the tallest man I'd ever seen, and she walked over to me. She reached out her hand, which was like a human's, but her fingers were longer, and the back of her hand was hairy.

"I don't think I even hesitated. I took her hand, and she led me over to the anthill and showed me what she was doing. Licking the stick to make it sticky—though sticks are always sticky, I guess—" Mack said with a chuckle, "and then sliding it down into the anthill. When she'd bring it up, ants would be crawling all over it. Then she'd lick them off the stick and do it again.

"Pretty soon, I had found my own stick, and we were taking turns."

"You ate live ants?" Uchenna asked.

"Yup, Sings Real Sweet. I don't remember how they tasted so much as how they felt crawling around in my mouth."

Elliot suddenly looked ill.

"Then I started playing tag with the child sasquatch. She'd poke me with a stick, and I'd poke her with mine. We chased each other around the gully, trying to poke each other. Once, she stepped on the male sasquatch's fingers. He grabbed her and threw her across the clearing. I got scared for

a moment. But she just pushed herself up with her knuckles, brushed the pine needles out of her long, soft hair, and started chasing me again."

"It sounds like heaven," Uchenna said softly.

"That's just how it felt, Sings Real Sweet. Anyway, after a long time, I got tired. I curled up next to the female who'd taught me how to eat ants, and I must have fallen asleep.

"Meanwhile, though, my parents were going crazy. They'd gotten back to our village and realized I wasn't with them. Night was falling and it was getting colder.

"Grandmother Moon was bright and high above the treetops, so they searched by her light. Hours and hours they looked for me. At last, one of the searchers saw something strange. Cedar bark had been piled up on top of an old hollow stump, making a sort of roof. When the searcher looked inside that hollow stump, there I was. Dry moss had been packed all around me to keep me warm, and I was fast asleep.

"Ever since, I've had a special bond with those big hairy guys. I've never gotten to play with them again like that. But when we see each other, we know we're family."

CHAPTER FIFTEEN

Professor Fauna said, "Mack, I like this story very much. But will you tell us why we were summoned here so urgently?"

"Right," Mack said, clapping his hands together. "It's like this. My family and I have been protecting the sasquatch for generations now, working as hard as we can to keep them secret. We remember what happened to the grizzlies when outsiders learned they were here.

"So, we were doing a pretty good job of

protecting the hairy fellas. The sasquatch mostly live in the valley down there, which is why Raven and I call it Sasquatch Valley. Whenever a film crew came to try to make a documentary about the sasquatch, we would confuse them by putting on the sasquatch suits, running in different directions, that sort of thing."

"That must be fun," Uchenna interrupted.

Raven grinned. "Super fun. Those camera guys get so worn-out."

Mack went on. "But things got harder when my wife . . . when my wife . . ." He trailed off and looked into his lap.

Raven patted his arm. "It's okay, Pop." She looked at the professor and the children. "My mom died last winter."

Mack nodded. "Since then, it's just been Raven and me. My brothers were here for a while, but Jack and Zack are in the marines, deployed overseas. And our other brother Dack is off in Hawaii, studying oceanography."

Uchenna and Elliot stole a glance at each other, but didn't want to interrupt.

"Yeah." Mack smiled. "We're Mack, Jack, Zack, and Dack. I can only imagine what would have happened if my parents had more boys: Slack? Shack? Lack? That would have been whack, let me tell you."

Raven groaned at her dad's bad joke. But behind her big, black-rimmed glasses, she looked quietly happy to see her father joking around.

"Without my wife," Mack went on, "Raven has had to do even more work around here, in addition to her schoolwork and the work of just

growing up—which isn't easy, I know. But she's tough, and we worked hard, and things were going okay."

"So what happened?" Elliot asked.

"The Schmoke brothers happened," Mack replied.

Professor Fauna let out a growl from deep in his throat. Jersey looked up at the sound and growled, too.

"Again?" Elliot sighed, throwing up his arms. "Why is it always them?"

"Wherever mythical creatures are threatened, it always seems to be them!" Uchenna agreed.

"Yup," Mack said, nodding. "Where there's Schmoke, there's fire."

Raven groaned again. Mack winked at her.

"The Schmoke brothers signed a deal with the tribal council to do some selective logging. Those big trees down in Sasquatch Valley are worth thousands of dollars each. A little bit of logging isn't a bad thing, if you do it responsibly.

I mean, he who lives in a log house shouldn't throw chain saws, right?" Mack said, jerking a thumb back at the carved poles behind him. "But I've got a secret source in the Schmoke organization that says they've got different plans."

"What source?" Raven asked. "You know someone who works for the Schmoke brothers?!" She was incredulous. "Not a member of the Muckleshoot, right?!"

"I can't talk about it, Raven. Too dangerous for all involved."

But Raven wasn't giving up. "Because no one from our tribe should work for them, even if they did sign a contract with the council. Their environmental record is awful!" Raven stopped. "Wait . . . or is your source Jesse Bob? Did he hack their email? Or is Officer Joe watching their offices? Did Nancy Bill get someone talking? She's good at that. . . ."

But Mack just set his jaw and looked down at

his daughter. Raven glared right back up at him through the large lenses of her black glasses.

"Anyway," Mack went on, "based on the information from my source—whatever or whoever it is—I'm pretty sure that the Schmokes aren't planning to do selective, responsible logging. With the amount of machinery they're bringing in, they could level the entire forest in a couple of weeks. Once they get those machines running, Sasquatch Valley could be clear-cut before the tribal council has time to get a court injunction to stop them."

"That's horrible!" Raven said. "And if the forest is gone—what happens to the sasquatch families?"

They all sat in silence, letting that sink in.

"What doesn't make any sense, though," Mack went on, "is that this logging scam isn't the only thing that's going on. Just when the Schmokes started negotiating with the tribal council, hordes of film crews and news crews and Bigfoot hunters descended on this area. Raven and I have been running around like crazy trying to lead them away from Sasquatch Valley, but there's only two of us. And I've got a lot to do to stay on top of this information source, so the Schmokes can't surprise us."

"And what did you say the source was again?" Raven asked very sweetly.

"I didn't," said Mack. He turned to Professor Fauna, Elliot, and Uchenna. "What I will say, though, is that we need help."

Professor Fauna spread his hands in front of him. *"Amigo mío,* that is why we are here. What can we do?"

Mack replied, "I need you all to learn how to help Raven with these film crews and Bigfoot hunters."

"Wait," said Uchenna, cocking her head and glaring at Mack. "Are you saying you're going to keep working on your secret angle with the

Schmokes, while we dress up in those Bigfoot costumes and run around the forest?"

Mack looked taken aback. "Well—"

"Because that sounds awesome," Uchenna concluded.

Mack laughed. "Okay, Sings Real Sweet. Raven's gonna take you guys out and show you a few things you need to know about the woods—tracking, navigating, that kind of thing."

Elliot started to nibble at his fingernails.

"Don't worry, boyfriend," Raven said. "I'll keep you safe."

Elliot nodded uncertainly at the Muckleshoot girl with the big glasses and the mischievous smile.

"And while you do that," Mack went on, "I'll figure out how to expose the Schmokes' plan. Schmoke 'em out, you might say."

"Mr. gəqidəb, do you make bad puns all the time?" Uchenna asked.

"Only when he's awake," Raven replied.

Fauna clapped his hands once. "It is a plan!" he said. "Fellow members of our noble society, let us now learn how to become Bigfeets!"

"And march to victory—on de feet!" Mack added.

Everyone groaned.

CHAPTER SIXTEEN

Mack dropped them all off at a large wooded park. The idea was that Raven would help them practice woodland skills and teach them how they'd work together to bamboozle the hunters and reporters, while Mack followed up on his mysterious source of information. When the sun was two hands higher in the sky—two hours later—he'd be back to pick them up.

Raven led Elliot, Uchenna, and Professor Fauna between the tall ocher trunks of the cedar trees, with pale green needles filtering the sunlight overhead. Jersey, who grew up among pines, scrabbled joyfully from tree to tree, clambering up the trunks with his claws and then gliding down on his red wings. Raven said he looked like a flying squirrel—except mostly blue. She pointed out holes in the trees where flying squirrels were sleeping until nightfall.

"I can't believe squirrels can fly," Uchenna murmured.

"I can't believe you have a Jersey Devil for a sidekick. . . ," Raven replied, "and you named him Jersey."

Uchenna laughed. "Right? Bonechewer is much better."

"I don't know." Raven watched him glide from one tree trunk to another. "I might have gone with Floating Death."

"AWESOME!" Uchenna crowed.

"You guys are weird," said Elliot.

Raven knelt down. "Anyway, let's get to it. My mom was the expert tracker and survivalist. But she taught me a lot before she passed. Out here in the forest, I know her spirit is with me." She took a deep breath and closed her eyes. When she opened them again, they were clear and purposeful. "Reading the forest is like reading a book," she said. "Everything you see gives you information about what's going on out here. Close your eyes."

They all closed their eyes.

"Okay, open them." Raven was standing a few yards away, pointing to a pile of round brown balls on the ground. They looked like chocolate candies.

"See these?" she said. "You can tell this is deer scat because it looks like a pile of

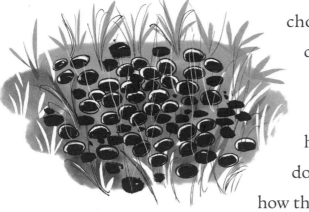

chocolate-covered caramels." Elliot and Uchenna came over to her as she knelt down. "Let's see how they taste." Raven picked one up and popped it into her mouth.

Elliot's eyes bulged. He felt like he was going to throw up. Uchenna wanted to look away, but couldn't. It was too disgusting.

Then Raven cracked a sideways grin. She took an empty candy box out of her pocket. "They look like chocolate because they are chocolate."

Elliot and Uchenna exhaled and laughed—but just then Professor Fauna, who was standing at another tree a short distance away, called out, "Children, I found some, too!" He was holding a small brown ball between his fingers. He popped it into his mouth. He chewed it thoughtfully.

"These do not taste at all like chocolate, actually," he said.

Raven cocked her head curiously and pointed at a brown pile by the professor's shoes. "That's because you're eating actual deer scat right now. . . ."

"Am I really? Interesting!" the professor replied. He continued chewing.

The kids stared at him, horrified.

CHAPTER SEVENTEEN

Raven made a small pile of rocks. "We have lots of ways to send messages without writing. Like tree-knocking, which is hitting tree trunks with sticks. Sasquatch do that to communicate with one another, too. And we can do this." She stood up and gestured down at her arrangement of stones. "See?"

"I get it!" Elliot said. "That sort of looks like an arrow. Does that mean to go in that direction?"

"ʔəsx̌əlabut čəxʷ," Raven said. It sounded like "us-ku-la-boot chuwh." "You got it, Screams A Lot. You're a fast learner. I think you're going to be okay when we're out on sasquatch patrol."

Raven smiling at him made Elliot feel warm and strange inside. He didn't like it. "Whatever. I'm sure I'll be eaten by a sasquatch."

"I think you'd taste disgusting to a sasquatch," Uchenna replied.

"Yeah," Raven agreed. "They'd probably just crush you to death."

"Ah, right," said Elliot. He felt comfortable again.

Uchenna spun around. "Hey, where's Professor Fauna?"

"Professor?" Elliot called.

"PROFESSOR!" all three of them called at once.

"SHHHH, BE QUIET!"

Fauna's whisper, which was louder than their calling, came from high in the rustling branches of a medium-size cedar tree. "COME UP HERE. QUIETLY! WE MUST NOT BE SEEN OR HEARD!"

The cedar's branches were as straight and evenly spaced as a ladder. Raven, Elliot, and Uchenna climbed up after Professor Fauna. They found the professor perched on a dangerously thin bough, with Jersey balancing on his shoulder. Both the professor and their tiny winged friend were peering through the branches toward the entrance to the park.

"You see?" Professor Fauna said, pointing with a long finger at the white van parked below.

"Oh no," Elliot said.

"Oh yes," Uchenna replied. "SNERT!"

"Bless you," said Elliot. Uchenna shot him a look and then focused on the Schmoke news van again.

Grace Goodwind stood near it, fixing her makeup and shaking out her long blond hair (in slow motion, somehow), as the cameraman got ready for an establishing shot.

"Bad news?" Raven asked.

Uchenna raised an eyebrow at her.

"Sorry," Raven apologized. "I guess my pop's punning is contagious."

"They are very bad news indeed," Fauna said. "Their company is owned by the Schmoke brothers."

Sam Brounsnout, the acne-faced producer, stood with his hands on his hips. They could just hear his voice in the distance. "The crazy truck-van-Cadillac thing definitely stopped here and dropped off that weird man and his kids."

"And that disgusting creature they had with

them," Grace added, smearing lipstick on her lips and smacking them together. "So, now we have to go in there and find them!"

"You're coming, too?" Andy the cameraman asked. "I'm surprised, Grace."

Grace winked at him. "One word, Mickey." She made her voice low and sultry. "Prime time."

"That's two words, Grace," said Andy.

"Don't talk back to the talent!" Grace snapped. Then she straightened her bright blue dress and made like she was in a shampoo commercial a few more times.

Professor Fauna turned and whispered to the kids, "They must not see us! We must be poised like the panther! Silent like the snake! Undercover like the oranguta—AHH!"

As he shifted on his branch, the professor's feet slipped. He would have fallen out of the tree if all three children had not grabbed him.

"There!" Grace shouted, pointing into the trees. "GO!"

CHAPTER EIGHTEEN

Andy the cameraman and Sam Brounsnout took off running, with Grace following after them, trying not to tumble over in her stiletto heels.

A moment later, they were in the park, staring up into the very cedar tree where the Unicorn Rescue Society was hiding. Uchenna had a tight grip on Professor Fauna. Elliot had a tight grip on Jersey. Raven had a tight grip on Elliot, which made Elliot feel very weird.

"Don't move," Raven whispered.

Andy focused his camera on the tree. "Can you see them?" he asked.

"No . . . ," Sam said, peering into the dense green branches.

"They've got to be up there," Grace snapped. "What kind of bird sings like an old man shrieking?"

"Who is calling Mito Fauna an old—" Professor Fauna tried to shout, but Uchenna shushed him.

"All right, Gilbert, camera on me!" Grace announced. "If we can't find the news, we'll make it."

"Gilbert?" Andy murmured. He trained his camera on Grace.

"This park may look peaceful," said Grace Goodwind, flipping her blond hair over her shoulder and training her cobalt eyes on the camera lens. "But in this tree behind me there is a horrible, terrible monster—one undiscovered by science. And we at SNERT will be the first to expose it to the world. Don't change that channel! We'll be here all day if we have to. The truth will be revealed! I'm Grace Goodwind and you can trust me to tell you all the news I want you to know."

She lowered her mic. "Sam, do you know how to operate a chain saw?"

"What?!?"

"Go buy a chain saw and we'll cut this dumb tree down!"

"This is a public park! And I've never used a chain saw in my life!"

"Then make sure it comes with an instruction

manual. We'll figure it out. Martin, keep that camera loaded!"

"It's digital, Grace. It's always loaded. And it's Andy."

"Whatever. Sam, what are you waiting for?"

Sam Brounsnout looked conflicted.

Just then, Uchenna whispered to Raven. "Do you have any more of those chocolates?"

"Sure. But you're hungry now?"

"Just give me one."

Raven reached into her pocket, brought out a chocolate-covered caramel, and handed it to Uchenna. Uchenna held it out in her hand and offered it to Jersey. He licked it into his mouth. Then he started whining for another one.

"What'd you do that for?" Elliot whispered. "Now he won't be quiet till he eats them all!"

"Can I have the rest?" Uchenna asked Raven. Reluctantly, Raven took the box out of her pocket and handed it over. Uchenna turned the camouflage backpack—which had air holes for

Jersey—around to her
stomach, opened it,
and dumped the can-
dies into the bottom.
Immediately, Jersey
scrambled from El-
liot's arms into the
backpack. "Stay quiet,
little buddy," Uchenna
whispered. And then, hoist-
ing Jersey's pack onto her back and turning to the
others, she said, "Follow my lead."

Uchenna began climbing down the tree.
Raven, Elliot, and Professor Fauna looked at one
another uncertainly. But they followed her.

Uchenna leaped to the ground from a low
branch, in front of the surprised SNERT crew.
"You got us," Uchenna said, as the other three
clambered down beside her. "Our teacher here is
trying to show us how to move stealthily in the
woods. But I guess we have more work to do."

"Where is that creature?!" Grace Goodwind exclaimed. "Rafael, roll 'em!"

"They're rolling, Grace," Andy muttered, his camera trained on the kids.

"What creature?" said Uchenna.

"That disgusting winged thing that you had in the burger joint! It looked like a blue baby deer crossed with a bat!"

Uchenna looked at Elliot, who looked at Raven, who looked at the professor. They all shrugged. Then Uchenna looked at Sam and gestured at Grace. "Does she have a problem or something?"

Sam stammered, "Well, I thought I saw something, too . . . but it does seem far-fetched, now that you mention it—"

"I know what I saw!" Grace snapped. Then her eyes narrowed. "What's in the bag?"

"Uh, nothing!" Elliot said at once. "Schoolwork!"

At the very same moment, Raven said, "Video games!"

They looked at one another awkwardly.

Professor Fauna, eager to help, said, "Of course! Because our school is a . . . uh . . . a school of video games! The International, uh, Video Game, uh, Academy and University! Yes!"

Grace looked skeptical. "And why does a video game academy and university, whatever that is, have classes in a tree?"

"Uh . . . ," Professor Fauna stammered.

"Um . . . As practice for playing our favorite game, of course! Which is called . . . which is called . . ."

"Ninjas in a Tree?" Raven offered.

Grace put a hand on her hip and raised an eyebrow. "I'm a reporter, guys. I can tell when people are lying to me."

"Except when they're politicians," said Sam Brounsnout.

"Except when they're politicians," agreed Grace Goodwind.

Uchenna replied, "I'm sorry, miss, you're right. My friends were lying. There's nothing in the bag but candy—my friends just don't want to share it with you. Here. Look." And Uchenna swung the bag around to her stomach and opened it.

Raven, Elliot, and Professor Fauna gasped.

Grace Goodwind, eyes wide, peered into Uchenna's backpack. Sam looked over her shoulder, and Andy trained the camera into the darkness of the bag.

There was clearly nothing in the bag. Nothing but some loose chocolate-covered caramels.

Then Uchenna said, "You guys need to find something better to do than follow some kids around with a camera. Isn't there some real news to cover?"

Sam stammered. Andy chortled and then tried to stifle it in his sleeve. But Grace said, "It must still be up in that tree! We're going to wait right here, as long as we have to. Wilbur, camera on me!"

"Wilbur? Really?" said Andy. "Whatever you say, Grace." He sighed.

Uchenna, Elliot, Raven, and Professor Fauna walked down the marked path and out into the sunny parking lot.

"Where'd he go?" Raven hissed.

"What do you mean?" Uchenna replied. She held the backpack open in the sunlight. A shimmering blue Jersey Devil was curled up in the bottom of the bag, devouring chocolate-covered caramels.

Raven's mouth fell open. Professor Fauna smiled proudly.

"Jersey Devils can turn invisible in the shade," Elliot explained. "That was some quick thinking, Uchenna."

She winked at him and zipped the backpack closed again, so Jersey could enjoy his candy in peace.

CHAPTER NINETEEN

Twenty minutes later, they were rumbling down the road in the TruckVanAc, the kids having just recounted their adventure with the SNERT reporters to Mr. gǝqidǝb.

"And you, *amigo mío*?" Professor Fauna asked Mack. "Have you found a way to expose the Schmoke brothers' villainous plans to clear-cut these forests?"

"Not quite yet," Mack replied. "But I discovered that Edmund and Milton Schmoke themselves are in town now. What you lot need to worry about," Mack said, jerking his thumb over his shoulder to the back of the TruckVanAc, "is fitting into those sasquatch suits."

Uchenna picked up a hot, hairy costume. "It smells," she said.

"More believable that way," Raven answered. She held up the hard hat and orange vest that Elliot had deposited on the floor. Under the hard hat she saw a blond wig. "Dad, what is all this?"

Mack looked quickly at what his daughter was referring to, then he retrained his vision back at the road and changed the subject. "We'll hike into Sasquatch Valley," Mack said, "carrying our costumes in our packs. Raven and I will show you the lay of the land. Then we'll put on our big feet, start laying down false trails, let ourselves get seen from a distance by some of those film crews, and try to keep them away from the heart of the valley."

It was an hour's hike from Mack's house to the trail. Along the way, Elliot and Uchenna marveled at the abundance of green life around them, the way the trees were covered with moss, the gray beard lichen hanging down from the branches of the old firs. They heard the two sharp, clear notes of a white-crowned sparrow, and as they reached a small brook, stopped for a while to watch little birds diving off the stones to disappear underwater and reemerge with insects in their beaks.

"There's so much here," Mack said. His voice was quiet as he spoke. "And it all depends on these big, beautiful life-givers, the trees. Creatures of all sorts and sizes rely on them. Not just the big ones, like sasquatch. So many birds. There's juncos, sparrows, pine siskins, cross-bills, all eating the seeds. Then there's the little mammals, like that guy there."

Elliot looked in the direction Mack was pointing. A tiny

red-furred creature scurried around a massive tree trunk.

"Red tree vole?" Elliot asked.

"Good eyes, little buddy. Then there's the bigger Douglas squirrel, shrews, mice, chipmunks, flying squirrels. They all use the cavities in the old trees for nests. Cut down these trees and . . . you just destroyed their whole world."

As they continued, Elliot kept using his eyes to pick out the clues left by forest creatures. It was like reading a book. And Elliot was a champion reader.

"Deer tracks," he said. "Maybe a doe and one—no, two—fawns!"

"Good eyes again," Mack said, flashing him a thumbs-up. "We might just have to give you a new nickname. What about that there?"

Elliot studied the parallel scratches on the bark of a tree. He knew what they were! And to his own surprise he wasn't scared—just excited.

"Bear clawings, right? It reached up as high as it could to make those."

"Yup, marking its territory. If another bear comes along and can't reach up that high, he'll figure he'd better leave."

"Mr. gəqidəb," Uchenna said. "Excuse me, but it seems as if you're not making any silly jokes now. Like you didn't say it was 'too much to bear' or he could 'bearly reach that high.'"

Mack smiled. "That's right, Uchenna—though those are good ones. I'll have to remember them." He looked around. "When I'm here in these woods, I don't feel the need to make jokes. I just want to feel the spirit of everything around us."

As they took the trail that led down into the valley, there were places where huge trees had fallen across their path. They had to either crawl under or over them.

"Poor trees," Uchenna said, after they clambered over the third one.

"No," Raven said. "It's just that their time came

to fall. All sorts of plants and animals and birds are still using them. One day they'll be part of the soil, feeding other trees. They're still here in the woods, a part of it all." She paused. "Like my mom."

Mack stopped, looked back at his daughter, and smiled sadly.

Meanwhile, Uchenna had picked up a dead branch that was shaped like a big drumstick. She tapped it against the trunk of a big dead tree that was still standing, stripped of its bark. It made a hollow thump like a drum.

BUM BUM BUM

"How cool is this!?" she exclaimed. She began tapping harder in a complicated rhythm.

"Uh . . . ," said Raven.

DADABUM DADABUM

"Um, Uchenna," the professor said. "That may not be a good idea."

"But, listen," Uchenna said, knocking out another rhythm. "Dig the acoustics on this!"

DA BUM DA BUM
DADADADA BUM

"Yes," Mack said. "It does echo far. That's why you should stop."

Uchenna stopped and looked up at Mack. "I don't understand."

"That's how sasquatch send messages to one another. Remember?" Raven reminded her.

"Right!" said Elliot. "Maybe, if we communicate with them, we can warn them about the danger!"

Raven shook her head. "Maybe, boyfriend, and maybe not. That rhythm Uchenna was pounding out might just be a message—or it may have been like those bear marks on that tree back there. A challenge!"

Suddenly, a huge roar, louder than the drumming, shook the forest.

The leaves on the trees trembled. When the roar died away, the echo lingered.

Professor Fauna grabbed the stick from Uchenna and pushed himself in front of her. "It sounds like, maybe, it was a challenge," he whispered.

For a moment, everything was silent.

And then, with a crashing of brush and branches, an eight-foot-tall sasquatch stomped out from behind a tree. It had beautiful silken hair, long and brown, and a face like an ape's. In one swift motion, before anyone could move, it scooped up the professor in one of its enormous furry hands and dangled him upside down from one leg.

At which point Elliot did the only logical thing he could think to do.

He screamed.

CHAPTER TWENTY

Elliot's scream was, not surprisingly, louder than usual. It was so piercing that the sasquatch let go of the professor's leg and clapped its palms over its ears. The professor landed in a pile at the giant's huge feet, and then he scrambled to get away. But the sasquatch put one big hairy foot on top of him, pinning him to the ground.

Raven grabbed Elliot and put her hand over his mouth.

"Quiet," she whispered. "Don't scream again. If you do, the professor might get stomped."

The sasquatch lowered its hands from its ears. It scowled down at the humans.

"Don't make eye contact," Mack whispered. "Look toward the ground."

"How can I do so?" the professor wheezed. "Its big foot . . . is on top of . . . my face."

Uchenna said to Mack, "We have to save him!"

"Shhh," said Mack. He raised his left hand slowly, and then pressed his palm over his heart.

The sasquatch watched Mack's sign. Its face softened. It began to lift its foot from the professor's face.

But just then, a small creature came gliding out of the sky and landed on the hirsute primate's long arm.

"Jersey!" Uchenna cried. The sasquatch's weight shifted back onto its foot. The professor made a sound like his head was being crushed. Which it was. The sasquatch lifted its huge hand to flatten Jersey like a human would crush a mosquito.

"No!" Elliot cried.

But instead of crushing him, the sasquatch's hand slowed, and then gently began to pet Jersey's head. The scowl left the hairy giant's face.

It lifted its foot off Fauna's head.

"Huh. I think she likes Jersey," murmured Raven.

"How do you know it's a she?" Uchenna asked.

A sound came from the bushes to their right. Three more sasquatch came out—one a bit shorter than Elliot, one the same height as Uchenna, and one slightly taller than Raven.

"I think that's their mom," Raven whispered.

The sasquatch children looked shyly at the humans, and then up at their mother. She walked over to them and then sat down, heavily, on the ground. Jersey stayed perched on her shoulder.

The humans watched as the three sasquatch children crowded around Jersey, petting his head and stroking his wings. He purred and licked their faces.

And then, Jersey scrambled to the forest floor and over to Elliot. He scurried up Elliot's pant leg and shirt, and perched on top of his head.

"Uh . . . ," said Elliot. "What is he doing?"

No one answered him. The sasquatch children were gazing curiously at Jersey—and at Elliot. Slowly, they started to move toward him.

"Uh . . . guys?" Elliot said.

The three sasquatch kids moved into a circle around Elliot.

"Any advice?" Elliot asked. "Mr. gəqidəb? Raven? Anyone?"

The sasquatch kid standing right in front of Elliot motioned with a hand. Elliot stared. She motioned again. It looked like the sasquatch child was telling him to sit down.

"Uh, Mr. gəqidəb, what is going on?" asked Elliot.

"Sasquatch talk to one another with sign language," Mack replied. "All apes do—and a lot of the signs are the same across the ape and human family. You were born understanding many of the same signs that they use."

"So, what is she saying?" Elliot asked. He wasn't sure why he thought this sasquatch kid was a she, but he did.

"What do you think she's saying?" Mack asked. The sasquatch did the hand motion again.

"I think she's telling me to sit down."

"So do it, boyfriend," Raven said.

Elliot sat down.

The circle of sasquatch children tightened around Elliot. He closed his eyes and tried to breathe calmly. Inside his head, he was thinking, What is happening? What are they going to do to me? Why is no one helping? Why is Jersey sitting on my head? Should I scream? Probably not. I want to scream. Maybe I will.

And then, the sasquatch girl lifted Jersey off Elliot's head. She held the little Jersey Devil in her arms and stroked him like he was a cat. Elliot began to get up. But the sasquatch girl made a hand signal that looked like "don't move." So Elliot didn't move.

A moment later, he felt delicate fingers touching his hair. His eyes went wide.

"What is happening?" he whispered.

Uchenna and Raven were watching, and started to giggle. Professor Fauna was still on the ground next to the sasquatch mother, but now they were sitting as if they'd been friends forever. Mack was crouching nearby, grinning.

"They're doing your hair," Uchenna said.

"WHAT?" Elliot cried.

This startled the sasquatch children. The sasquatch holding Jersey frowned and put her hand over her mouth. Elliot nodded. She nodded back. He nodded again. Then one of the sasquatch kids doing his hair grabbed his head to make him stop nodding and stay still.

Finally, the sasquatch mother stood up. The children stopped what they were doing. The girl holding Jersey kissed the top of his head—Uchenna's heart just about melted—and then handed Jersey back to Elliot. Then they turned and headed into the forest.

In an instant, the sasquatch family had disappeared.

None of the humans moved.

Then they all exhaled.

"Whoa!" Uchenna exclaimed. "That. Was. Awesome."

"Truly spectacular!" Fauna said, brushing himself off and picking pine needles from his beard. "How fine to see a family of them! All in such superb condition!"

"That was my friend," said Mack. When Elliot and Uchenna looked at him quizzically, he added, "Who chased me with a stick."

Uchenna said, "She's all grown up!"

"We both are," Mack agreed.

Professor Fauna turned to Elliot. "And the grooming they were doing! Elliot, you look *magnífico!*"

Long strands of pale green moss and twigs with tiny pinecone buds stuck every which way out of Elliot's curly mop of hair. Raven and Uchenna broke up in a fit of giggling.

Elliot sighed. "I wish I could see myself right now."

"No," said Raven, "you don't."

She and Uchenna laughed harder.

And then they stopped.

Mack had tapped them on their shoulders. "Look," he said.

An all-too-familiar blond woman was standing at the top of a nearby hill, waving her arms and shouting at her harassed-looking cameraman.

As the wind changed, her voice drifted down to them. "Randy, you idiot! What do you mean you missed the shot! You could have had a family of Bigfeet on camera and weren't set up yet?"

Andy was muttering something about batteries dying and his name being Andy and how he once knew a guy named Randy in middle school who was a real jerk and maybe he should just make a name tag for himself. Sam Brounsnout was nowhere to be seen.

"We've gotta lose them," Mack said. "Quick, follow me."

He didn't have to say it twice. Uchenna, Elliot, Raven, and the professor all ducked under the thick-needled branches onto a small trail that led into deep woods. They started to run. They ran and ran and ran, until Elliot's lungs were burning and Uchenna's feet felt like iron. Jersey glided from tree to tree above their heads.

Finally, Mack pulled up. "It's okay. We can stop now. No way they're going to catch up with us lugging that TV camera."

"Or in stilettos," Raven added, her shoulders rising and falling.

"Wait a minute," Uchenna said. "Where's Professor Fauna?"

Mack's head swiveled in one direction and then another. "Mito!" he called. "Mito?"

"Professor Fauna?"

"Professor Fauna!!!"

There was no answer. The founder of the Unicorn Rescue Society was gone.

CHAPTER TWENTY-ONE

Professor Fauna was not lost. He prided himself on never being lost. Even that time when he was wandering in the Amazon jungle for two weeks, half naked and nearly starving, he was far from lost. After all, wherever he went, there he was.

However, at the moment, as he wandered through the mossy forest, he did not know exactly where he was. Sadly, Elliot and Uchenna and Jersey and Mack and Raven were nowhere in sight. They were surely hopelessly lost and needed him to find them.

He also wondered where the sasquatch family had gone. He thought of finding another stick and striking it against a tree. That had worked wonderfully well for Uchenna. Then, as he entered a small clearing, he noticed a mass of something black and organic on the ground. Sasquatch fecal matter, perhaps?

Only one way to tell. He pried a piece off and tasted it. Disgusting. It was rotted fungus. But there was hope. Perhaps that squishier pile over there would prove to be poop.

As he was leaning over to stick his finger into that second interesting, odiferous heap, he heard a stick crack behind him. He turned to look. To his horror, it was a group of the most dangerous and deadly animals in the world.

Humans.

Emerging from the woods was a surveying crew from the logging company, carrying sextants and surveying rods. And then, behind them, emerged two men in sharp navy suits, one tall and thin, the other short and squat. Their eyes sparkled like cut gemstones, matching their tie clips—one emerald, the other sapphire. On their heads they wore yellow hard hats that almost concealed their bald domes.

It was, of course, the Schmoke brothers.

"You!?" Milton Schmoke, the taller of the two, exclaimed, when he saw Professor Fauna.

"Why are you everywhere we go?" Edmund Schmoke demanded.

Professor Fauna pulled himself up to his full, imposing height. "Because everywhere you go, you threaten the creatures of myth and legend! Your treachery and villainy know no bounds!" He turned to the surveying crew. "Did you know that these two men have captured dragons, threatened a Jersey Devil, endangered the world's mermaid population, and plan to make sasquatch extinct—"

"Men," Milton Schmoke cut in, "this man is a saboteur. He is obsessed with us, and obviously deranged. He can't be allowed anywhere near a Schmoke operation."

The head surveyor said, "So, you want us to—"

"GET HIM!" Edmund shouted.

Quick as a cobra, Professor Fauna pulled off his left shoe and raised it above his head like a club. "Stay back!" he shouted. "I am armed . . . or, maybe, footed!"

The surveyors hesitated. He didn't look dangerous, but he did look a little unhinged.

"NOW!" Edmund admonished them.

Four burly men in hard hats rushed the professor. He smacked one in the face with his shoe, but the others quickly grabbed his arms and legs. He struggled, but their hands were strong as tree roots.

"Tie him up," Milton said.

The lead surveyor took some orange cord from his utility belt, and the men bound the professor's hands and feet. Then they dragged him behind them as they continued on their way. Professor Fauna struggled at first, but soon he found that it was of no use. He had been captured.

CHAPTER TWENTY-TWO

After some time, the group of surveyors, led
by the Schmoke brothers and dragging Professor Fauna behind them, reached a road. The
surveyors' truck and a black Humvee with tinted
windows stood by the side of the road and, parked
behind those, the SNERT van. Grace Goodwind
and her cameraman were nowhere in sight, but
Sam Brounsnout was there, nervously pacing
back and forth.

Seeing the Schmokes, he hurried up to them.

"Sir! And, sir! Mr. Milton, Mr. Edmund! It is so good to see you." He held out his hand. Milton waved him off.

"Chairs," Milton growled.

"Now, Brounsnout!" Edmund added.

Sam caught sight of the hog-tied professor, who had been dropped on the ground by the surveyors. He hesitated for just a moment, before thinking better of saying anything. He quickly produced two folding chairs for the Schmoke brothers.

"Phipps!" Milton called.

Instantly, their faithful butler, Phipps, appeared, wearing his customary black suit, carrying a tray of cookies, cups, and a teapot.

"Report, Brounsnout!" Milton said, as Phipps handed the two brothers a cup of tea and plate of cookies each.

"Mmmph," Edmund added, stuffing a cookie into his mouth.

"Wonderful news!" The producer beamed.

"Grace Goodwind and our cameraman had a sighting. They're closing in on a real Bigfoot family!"

"Sasquatch! They are sasquatch!" the professor shouted from where he lay. No one paid him any attention.

"Excellent!" Edmund exclaimed, spraying cookie crumbs from his mouth. "Give Phipps their location. Phipps, take these surveyors with you. Subdue the Bigfoot family. Use the nets and tranquilizer guns. We want them alive. Don't let any of our goons kill them until we've extracted what we need."

Sam Brounsnout, who was suddenly very confused, watched Phipps and the five surveyors prepare their gear, including the tranquilizer guns. A very tall surveyor with bushy blond hair shoved down his hard hat and glared in Professor Fauna's direction.

"Mr. Milton, Mr. Edmund, I don't understand," Sam said. "Capture them? Kill them? What about our live broadcast? The first confirmed sighting of Bigfoot! Think of the ratings!"

Edmund laughed. "Hah! Ratings? Who cares about that? Our aim was to locate and capture them, not share them with the world. You won't be telling anyone about what you've seen here. Have you read the nondisclosure agreement you signed? It was very thorough."

"Try telling anyone what color socks you're wearing today," Milton said through a mouthful of cookies. "Our lawyers will sue you so ruthlessly your children's children will be destitute."

"But we're a news station! Why did you send us here if you don't want it broadcast?"

"Fool!" Milton sneered. "The same reason we hired half the Bigfoot hunters and documentarians in the country. The good thing about reporters is that they can be excellent at finding the truth."

"And the bad thing about reporters," Edmund added, "is that then they want to share it. That is unacceptable. And that is why we started this little news network, so we can only share as much truth as we want people to know. You will not broadcast any encounter with the Bigfeet."

"They are sasquatch!" Fauna shouted again, though he was being ignored even more than before, if that was possible. "They are not—" His words were cut short as a large hand was clamped over his mouth. He looked around frantically in an attempt to figure out who was muffling him, but he couldn't see whoever it was. The surveyors

were still walking around the site, carrying their tranquilizer guns.

"Catching those Bigfoots is all we care about," Milton said. "That is why we entered into that contract with those credulous Indians. Because once we level the whole forest, the Bigfoots will have nowhere to hide."

"Bigfeet," his brother corrected him.

"No, Edmund, I'm rather sure it's Bigfoots."

"But . . . but why?" Sam Brounsnout asked.

"But why?" Edmund mimicked him. "It is not for you to ask why. We pay, you obey. Those are the rules."

Sam stared at the brothers in disbelief.

Whoever had clamped a hand over Professor Fauna's mouth was now dragging him, quietly, toward the forest. The surveyors barely noticed, and the Schmokes didn't notice at all. The professor considered trying to shout for help—except that someone seemed to be kidnapping him from his kidnappers. Which he figured was a good thing? Or was it? He wasn't entirely—

"Don't worry, Mito," a voice whispered into his ear. "I recorded it all the traditional Indian way—on my phone."

CHAPTER TWENTY-THREE

A s Professor Fauna was dragged out of sight, the Schmokes drank their afternoon tea, while Phipps and four heavily muscled survey-ors loaded themselves and their guns into the surveyors' truck.

Sam Brounsnout stood still as a Douglas fir, lost in thought. *What would Walter Cronkite have done?* he asked himself.

Then, a light went on in the young produc-er's brain. He set his jaw, straightened his back, stepped up into the news van, and closed the door behind him.

The sound of the door slamming and the click of its lock caught the attention of Milton and Edmund Schmoke. They watched as the satellite dish on top of the vehicle began rising into position.

"What is happening, Edmund?" Milton cried.

"He is preparing to broadcast!" Edmund cried back.

"We must stop him! No news is good news! Where are our muscle monkeys?" Milton shouted. "Phipps! Where have you and our leg-breaking goons gone off to?"

There was no reply, of course. Phipps and the burly brutes, now heavily armed, had already roared off in the truck.

Edmund banged on the door of the van. "Brounsnout, open this door or we shall terminate your employment immediately."

"In other words, you're fired!" Milton shouted.

A window near the top of the van opened briefly.

"I don't care!" the producer called down to them. "I went to journalism school! I want to bring the world the truth! The whole planet is gonna see Bigfoot! And you two can kiss my snout!" He slammed the window shut. Then he opened it again, just long enough to crow, "Stay tuned!" Then he slammed it shut again.

As the window clicked closed, the two brothers stared at each other.

"I thought you said he would do anything for money," Milton said.

"He had been working at Ferret News before he got this job, so I just figured . . . ," Edmund mumbled. He brought out a gold-plated smartphone and logged on to the SNERT website. The image of Grace Goodwind's perfectly made-up face filled the screen:

"Grace Goodwind reporting live from the tribal lands of the . . . where are we again, Fabio? Oh, right . . . live from the tribal lands of the Muckleshoot Indian Nation in the Pacific Northwest. Exciting breaking news! I, Grace Goodwind, of the Schmoke News, Entertainment, and Retail Television network, am about to prove beyond any doubt that a creature from dumb old myths and stories is actually REAL!"

As the newswoman extended her arm to point behind her, the image shifted to

the forest, zooming in on three dark shapes
moving cautiously beneath the trees.

"There they are," Grace Goodwind
whispered, leaning in front of the lens so that
her face again filled the screen. "Not just one,
but three of them. Three young sassy catches."

"Sasquatch. The plural of sasquatch is
sasquatch," Andy whispered.

Grace Goodwind gestured that her
sound feed be cut—which it was not. "Quiet,
Flavius. You're the cameraman. I'm the
talent. Now turn my mic back on."

Flipping her hair back and opening her eyes wide, she again addressed the camera: "There they are, baby sassy crutches, shown at last to America and the world. This is Grace Goodwind, reporting for SNERT— wait, who are those guys?"

Out of the woods, five men were emerging. Phipps and the surveyors.

"Oh no," Milton moaned. "Not on live TV!"

"Perhaps no one is watching," Edmund said.

The window on the top of the van popped

open again briefly. "Largest viewership in the history of SNERT right now," Sam Brounsnout

shouted down in a triumphant voice. "All the networks are picking it up!"

"Can we call our men off?" Milton asked.

"Too late now," Edmund moaned. "Look."

Indeed, on the tiny SNERT feed on Edmund's phone, things were happening at lightning speed.

"Get them," Phipps shouted. "In the name of Schmoke Industries and the Schmoke Logging Company!"

The four surveyors with tranquilizer guns and nets quickly encircled the trio of hairy creatures.

"What are those mean men going to do to those poor little sassy couches?" Grace Goodwind said in a horrified voice.

*"Sasquatch. The plural is—" the
cameraman whispered.*

"Shut up, Flaubert!"

*A struggle ensued, streamed live for
all the world to see: The Schmoke surveyors
grabbed the three juvenile sasquatch and tried
to wrestle them to the ground. The small
furry ones fought valiantly, striking out with
their fists and kicking the shins of the hard-
hatted attackers. But they were overpowered
and pinned to the mossy forest floor.*

"This is horrible publicity!" Edmund groaned as
Milton kept banging on the door of the van.

"Stop! Halt! Cease! Desist!" he yelled, but to
no avail.

*Then, as the horrified Schmokes and millions
of viewers watched, the camera zoomed in
for a close-up of the face of one of the small
sasquatch—and its head fell off.*

"AHHHHHH!" Grace Goodwind shrieked. "It's . . . Wait . . . Is that a . . ."

Indeed, it was. For when the false head was dislodged, it disclosed the sweaty, grinning face of Raven.

She looked directly at the camera. "Good afternoon, America," she said.

The Schmoke goons stepped back as the two other heads were removed by their wearers—Elliot and Uchenna.

"Oh no," Phipps groaned. "The masters will not be pleased. This was yet another hoax. Bigfoot, indeed!" He sighed. "Men, follow me."

As Phipps hurried off, followed by his chastened crew, the trio of costumed children stood up and waved at the camera.

Grace Goodwind ignored them.

"On me, Bob," she said to the cameraman. "And so, thanks to our fearless reporting, we now know beyond the shadow of a doubt that Bigfeets are nothing more

WHO OWNS THE MOON?
THE ANSWER MAY SURPRISE YOU

SNERT TV

than a meaningless prank. But now we have another mystery to unravel. Why would the employees of Schmoke Industries attack what appeared to be a harmless furry family? Stay tuned for my next explosive report!"

Edmund switched off his smartphone.

"She is so fired," Milton snarled. "SNERT is over!"

"Indeed," Edmund agreed. "If we had wanted journalism, we would never have started a cable news channel."

"We can still bring in our logging team and slash down this nasty forest—and make a healthy profit," Milton growled, waving his arms at the big trees around them. "We have our agreement with those credulous Muckleshoots."

"Oh, no you do not," a deep voice said.

The brothers turned to look.

One of the surveyors was standing there, hands on his hips.

"It appears to be one of our goons," Milton said.

"What's he doing here?" Edmund asked, puzzled. "Didn't he go with the others?"

"Allow me to disclose—by removing 'dese' clothes—my true identity," Mack gəqidəb said. He pulled off his hard hat, his orange vest, and his blond wig with a dramatic flourish.

"I still don't know who he is," Milton said to his brother. "Though I do like that wig."

"I'll tell you who he is, you vile miscreants!" Professor Fauna stepped out from behind a tree.

"Not you!" Edmund said. "We had you tied up!"

"My fine Muckleshoot friend freed me," Professor Fauna said, placing his hand on Mack's shoulder. "And he has also cleverly engineered your downfall! Show them, *amigo mío.*"

Mack held up his phone. "I videoed your speech about clear-cutting our forest. Sent it to the tribal chair. He wrote back pretty darn quick."

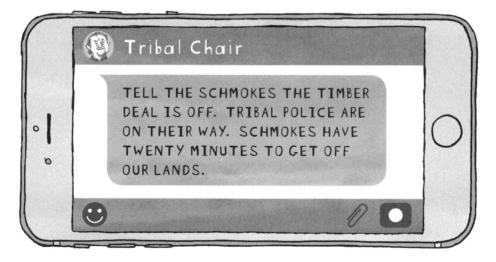

Tribal Chair

TELL THE SCHMOKES THE TIMBER DEAL IS OFF. TRIBAL POLICE ARE ON THEIR WAY. SCHMOKES HAVE TWENTY MINUTES TO GET OFF OUR LANDS.

Edmund shook his head, resigned. "Well, that is disappointing."

"Losing the lumber deal doesn't matter that

much, brother," Milton snarled. "Now that we know Bigfoot isn't real. We only wanted to clear the forest to catch him."

"But why?" Mack asked. "I don't get how you could hate sasquatch?"

"Hate?" said Milton. "We don't hate the Bigfeet!" He removed his own hard hat to reveal his hairless pate. "Our last encounter with the Unicorn Rescue Society left us hairless! And this cannot be! We are the world's handsomest billionaires!"

"Now the baldest . . . ," Edmund grumbled.

"By collecting the Bigfoots of the Pacific Northwest," Milton continued, "we were hoping to find a way to regrow our hair. DNA extraction, gland reproduction—"

"A huge collection of wigs . . . ," added Edmund.

"Whatever it took!" concluded Milton.

Just then, their huge black Humvee pulled up, piloted by Phipps. The Schmokes' henchmen began to climb out.

Fauna reached down to remove his shoe.

"Forget it," Edmund ordered their men, as a siren sounded from down the road. "The police are on their way. Come, brother. There are more fish in the sea."

"Yes, but do fish have hair?" Milton added, glaring at the professor.

He climbed into the vehicle, followed by his brother. The door slammed, and with a roar of the engine and a spinning of the tires, they were gone.

CHAPTER TWENTY-FOUR

As the night-black Humvee roared off, Elliot, Uchenna, and Raven emerged from the forest. No longer wearing their sasquatch gear, they looked like three normal kids returning from a hike through the woods. Except for the little Jersey Devil, floating from tree trunk to tree trunk above their heads. That was less normal.

"Children!" Professor Fauna shouted, opening his arms wide. "You have done magnificently well! Thanks to you and my good friend Mack, the phony Schmoke henchman, we have vanquished the Schmoke brothers yet again!"

"Are they gone for good?" Raven asked.

"They're gone for bad," Mack replied. "But I doubt that they'll ever come back here."

"I have a question," said Elliot.

"Why am I not surprised?" Mack chuckled.

"Why didn't you tell us that you were working as one of the Schmoke brothers' surveyors?" Elliot asked. "You didn't think you could trust us with the secret?"

Mack looked at the ground. "It wasn't that. It was that I hadn't told Raven that I was working for the Schmokes. I wasn't sure she would understand." He looked at Raven. "I know your mom would have been mad."

Raven shrugged. "It was all part of the plan, right?"

"It was, but I didn't know if you'd think it was worth it."

Raven smiled at her father. "I think you're a

hero." Mack suddenly rubbed something from the corner of his eye. "Speaking of heroes," Raven went on, "we did a pretty good sasquatch impersonation, didn't we, Pop?"

Mack furrowed his brow. "Well, things did look a little hairy for a while there. But when you took off your costume, you really pulled it off."

"Pop!" Raven groaned. Then she threw her arms around him.

"Seriously," Mack said, "I'm proud of you,

daughter. You and your friends did an amazing thing. Which is why, with Professor Fauna's permission, I'd like to give you something."

He held out his hand. On his broad palm sat a silver ring.

Raven looked closely. Inside a circle atop the ring was the raised design of a unicorn.

"Is this . . . ?" Raven asked, lifting the ring up to study it.

"Yes, daughter. It was your mother's. You know that every member of the Unicorn Rescue Society has one."

"We don't wear ours," Uchenna said, holding up her bare fingers. "Too conspicuous at school."

"Also, the ones the professor gave us were way too big," Elliot added.

"If you're giving this to me," Raven said, looking from her father to Professor Fauna, "that means . . ."

The professor pulled himself up to his full height and announced, in his most official-sounding voice, "We hereby make Raven ɡəqidəb an official member of the Unicorn Rescue Society!"

Raven gave a shout and jumped in the air. Then she spun toward Elliot. "Can you help me get it on?"

"Uh . . . okay . . . ," Elliot said, confused. But he took the ring from Mack's hand and slipped it onto Raven's finger.

"Perfect," Raven said. "Now we are legally engaged!"

Elliot's mouth fell open. Then Raven punched him in the arm. "Just kidding, boyfriend. I don't expect you to ask me to marry you until we are at least out of high school."

Elliot stammered for a moment. But then Raven said, "Look!"

Everyone turned. A large shape was making its way through the forest. The members of the Unicorn Rescue Society waited, barely breathing. And then the mother sasquatch emerged from the underbrush. She was carrying a thick fir branch, peeled clean. Her three children were standing all around her.

Jersey leaped from a nearby tree trunk and landed on the mother sasquatch's shoulder. She rubbed her hand against his blue cheek. The huge sasquatch turned her gaze to the members of the Unicorn Rescue Society. The corners of her wide mouth turned up. Then she looked to her children and flicked her hand at the humans.

The three little ones loped forward. Each one was carrying a small round stone.

"Hold out your hands," Mack said softly.

Uchenna, Raven, and Elliot did as he said. The sasquatch children dropped a small stone into each of their waiting palms. The stones were marked with a single spot of red berry juice.

"Awesome," Uchenna whispered. The stone still held the warmth of the sasquatch's hand.

"Do I also receive a present?" Professor Fauna asked.

Just then, the mother sasquatch hurled the heavy branch to the professor. The tree limb was so large that it knocked him down.

"*Muchas . . . gracias . . . ,*" the professor gasped, sitting on the ground under his gift.

The mother sasquatch, who still had Jersey on her shoulder, knelt down. The three sasquatch children came over to her and, one at a time, kissed Jersey on his little blue head. Then the mother sasquatch slid her hand under Jersey's belly and lowered him to the forest floor.

Then the sasquatch mother, followed by her little ones, turned and disappeared into the forest.

Mack helped the professor remove the heavy branch from his chest and rise to his feet. "I guess that was her way to thank you for going out on a limb."

All three children rolled their eyes. Professor Fauna admired his weighty gift. "*Bien.* This may serve as a walking stick," he said, attempting with little success to hold it with just one hand. And then he added, "For very, very short strolls."

CHAPTER TWENTY-FIVE

Just then, Elliot looked at his watch. "Oh no!" he exclaimed. "Professor, are we done here? I need to get home or my mom will kill me."

"We are done, indeed," Professor Fauna said. "But there is the small matter of obtaining transport. I am not sure the *Phoenix* is flight-worthy. In fact," he said, looking around, "I cannot quite recall where I left it."

"In pieces," Uchenna said, "scattered all over a forest in Oregon."

Elliot groaned. "I'm going to be grounded until I am seventy years old when I get back home. If I get back home."

"It's okay," Raven said. "You can stay with us!"

Elliot took a deep breath. He could feel a panic attack coming on.

"Folks," Mack said. "Come with me."

Everyone followed as Mack led them up past the bend where the forest trail joined the paved main road.

There, parked on the roadside, was Professor Fauna's small blue aircraft. Not only had it been pieced back together and furnished with new landing gear, the *Phoenix* looked finer than usual.

"*¡Mi querida avioneta! ¡Qué bonita quedaste!*" Professor Fauna cried, and he ran over to the plane and began to rub his hands along the *Phoenix*'s freshly re-painted fuselage.

"As soon as I saw you hit that treetop," Mack said, "I put in a call to a cousin of mine who works

at the Boeing plant outside Seattle. He patched it all up and delivered it here an hour ago. He just had one question for you, though."

"What is that?" the professor said, looking up from where he stood with his arms wrapped lovingly around the right wing.

"He wanted to know"—Mack grinned—"if this plane came from the same folks who make Legos."

Soon, Professor Fauna, Uchenna, Elliot, and Jersey were on board.

"We don't ever say good-bye in Muckleshoot,"

Mack said, a serious look on his face. He paused. "Instead we say toodle-oo."

"How does one pronounce that?" Fauna asked.

"Pop," Raven said, "get serious for just a minute, okay?"

Mack grinned again. "No, what we actually say is huy"—it sounded like "hoyt"—"which means something like 'the time we spent together is finished now.' But it might be better to just say the words for 'I will see you all later'—ɬuɫabdubuɬəd čəd."

"Tu lob doo bee seed?" Uchenna said.

"Close enough." Mack smiled.

Uchenna pulled the door closed, and Elliot strapped himself in as quickly as he could.

Outside the window, Raven shouted, "See you again, Screams A Lot! See you again, Sings Real Sweet! huy! ɬuɫabdubuɬəd čəd!"

"huy!" Uchenna and Elliot both yelled back.

The *Phoenix* picked up speed as it roared down the road. The professor pulled back on the controls. The plane rose like a kite into the sky. In no time at all, it was a small blue speck banking over the big trees, winging away from Sasquatch Valley, heading home to New Jersey.

ACKNOWLEDGMENTS

WE WOULD FIRST AND FOREMOST LIKE TO THANK the members of the Muckleshoot Indian Tribe who contributed so much to this book: Willard Bill, Jr., the tribe's cultural director, who kindly read the book, recommended a number of resources, and facilitated our interaction with the tribe; and Nancy Jo Bob, a Muckleshoot language expert, who was incredibly generous with her time throughout— from suggesting Muckleshoot terms to checking our implementation of the language in the text to coaching January LaVoy, our amazing audiobook reader, on the pronunciation of Muckleshoot words.

Major thanks are also due to Tami Hohn, a member of the Puyallup Tribe, for creating the beautiful SL Lushoot-seed Style True Type font used for the Muckleshoot words in this book.

Thanks to David Bowles, who ensured that Professor Fauna's Spanish is grammatical—and yet still as wacky as the professor is.

ADDITIONALLY, Joe would like to thank all of his friends in the Native communities of the Pacific Northwest who have always been so generous and helpful over the years.

AND FINALLY, Adam would like to thank Joe, for being an unparalleled storyteller, partner, and teacher through this process. Adam feels very humbled to have worked with such a legendary writer and such a legendarily painful punner. In all seriousness, the experience was series-changing and life-changing.

Joseph Bruchac is a *New York Times* bestselling author of over a hundred books, many of which draw on his Abenaki heritage. Although his northeastern American Indian heritage is only one part of an ethnic background that includes Slovak and English blood, those Native roots are the ones by which he has been most nourished. He continues to work extensively in projects involving the preservation of Abenaki culture, language, and traditional Native skills. Joe and his books have won numerous awards, including the Lifetime Achievement Award from the Native Writers Circle of the Americas.

ALTHOUGH THIS BOOK WAS A FUN PROJECT FOR ME and, I hope, will be fun for people to read, there are aspects to this story that I was very serious about.

The first was to make sure that we were not adding to any of the stereotypes about Native Americans in general or the Muckleshoot Tribal Nation in particular. As an indigenous person, I am always very concerned about this—especially when writing for young people.

That is why, from early on in the project, we relied not only on Native friends of mine from the Northwest and the experiences I've had there over several decades, but also turned directly to knowledgeable people in the Muckleshoot Nation itself. To say that they were warm and helpful is an understatement. This book would not be what it is without their input.

Further, though sasquatch may only be a legend to some people outside our indigenous communities, for many Native people throughout the continent this being is a reality and has a deep cultural and spiritual significance. Thus, in our portrayal, it was important to me that we show proper respect—while also, getting back to my opening sentence, having fun. Humor is a very large part of Native American cultures and I suspect that sasquatch get a chuckle out of us silly humans now and then, too.

—J.B.

Adam Gidwitz taught big kids and not-so-big kids in Brooklyn for eight years. Now he spends most of his time chronicling the adventures of the Unicorn Rescue Society. He is also the author of the Newbery Honor–winning *The Inquisitor's Tale,* as well as the bestselling *A Tale Dark and Grimm* and its companions.

Jesse Casey and **Chris Lenox Smith** are filmmakers. They founded Mixtape Club, an award-winning production company in New York City, where they make videos and animations for all sorts of people.

Adam and Jesse met when they were eleven years old. They have done many things together, like building a car powered only by a mousetrap and inventing two board games. Jesse and Chris met when they were eighteen years old. They have done many things together, too, like making music videos for rock bands and an animation for the largest digital billboard ever. But Adam and Jesse and Chris wanted to do something *together*. First, they made trailers for Adam's books. Then, they made a short film together. And now, they are sharing with the world the courage, curiosity, kindness, and courage of the members of the Unicorn Rescue Society!

Hatem Aly is an Egyptian-born illustrator whose work has been featured in multiple publications worldwide. He currently lives in New Brunswick, Canada, with his wife, son, and more pets than people. Find him online at metahatem.com or @metahatem.

PHOTO CREDIT: Michelle Pinet

Don't miss
the other adventures of

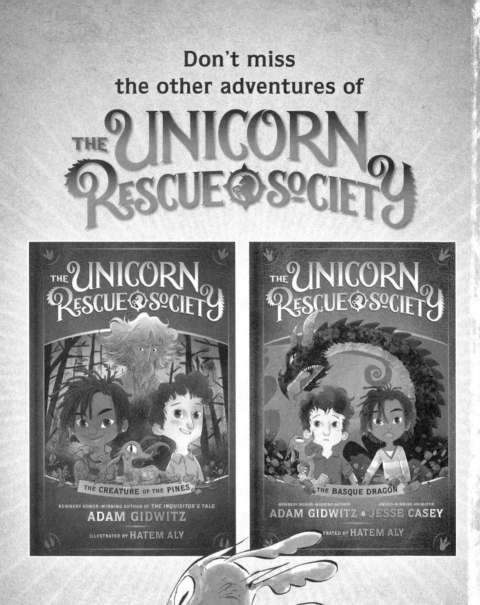